TIME

Eden Darry

Shannon is a young talented movie star celebrating the release of her new blockbuster. Jay is struggling to rebuild her life and hiding a dark secret. They meet and spend two nights together, forging a connection that neither can let go. With their lives heading in different directions, they agree not to stay in touch.

Ten years later, with their fortunes reversed, they meet again and neither has been able to forget the other. Will this time be different? Can they have a real chance at love? Or will Jay's secret and a tragic event pull them apart again?

Published by
NineStar Press
PO Box 91792
Albuquerque, New Mexico, 87199
www.ninestarpress.com

Warning: This book contains sexually explicit content and mentions of past rape and shooting death, which is only suitable for mature readers.

Print ISBN # 978-1-945952-63-0
Cover by Natasha Snow
Edited by Cora Walker

DEDICATION

For J, my beautiful girl

ACKNOWLEDGEMENTS

I'd like to say a massive thank you to Raevyn and everyone at Ninestar Press who made my private little daydream a reality. Thank you also to Natasha Snow who designs amazing covers—I've loved all of them. And Sera Trevor who proofread and gave me some very useful suggestions.

I'd especially like to thank Cora Walker, my editor, who always takes such care to make sure the story is as good as it can be. I'm incredibly fortunate to work with her.

CHAPTER ONE

March 2006

Jay didn't know what she was doing here. It definitely wasn't the kind of place she usually went. In here it was all shiny and tasteful, with its polished bar and the rows of expensive booze arranged perfectly on a glass shelf behind.

A huge chandelier hung from the ceiling in the centre, its crystal droplets catching the light and sparkling prettily like so many stars.

The places she had gone to before were dark and quiet, with the smell of stale beer and dirty carpets hanging thick. Nobody in those places paid any attention to anyone else, because when you weren't quite legal, you didn't want to be seen.

She sat at the bar, on a chrome and leather stool. The huge blackboard listed all kinds of wines and champagnes and cocktails with expensive sounding names. She tried to find one she'd heard of and couldn't.

Jay picked at the label on her bottle of Belgian beer and tried to pronounce the name but couldn't. She gave up and turned around on her stool, studying the clusters of beautiful people, dressed in chic clothes, all eerily clonelike as they quaffed exotic-looking cocktails, laughing a little too loudly and exposing perfect, blindingly white teeth. Just like the beer, these people were foreign to her. She'd been away a long time.

She sighed and wondered again why she had come here of all places. She took a long pull on her beer and tried to pronounce the name again.

* * *

Shannon Dempsey sighed and sipped her champagne. God, she was bored. Glancing around at her entourage, it dawned on Shannon she didn't like these people. Not one of them.

She'd been in London a couple of days to promote her new movie. Every night was the same: sat in the VIP area of some swanky London bar with people she didn't remember inviting.

They'd just kind of turned up at one point or another and stayed. *So-and-So was the girlfriend of someone else, who was friends with her hair stylist, and it was just so great to meet her, really, I just love your work. Champagne? Oh, thanks, don't mind if I do.* That was usually the way things went: a revolving door of faces that stuck around while the champagne was flowing and times were good. She knew how it worked, and she knew she had to sit and smile through it—smile until her face hurt.

She'd been in the movie business since she was fifteen. Plucked from obscurity out of a small town in Kansas, still in high school, and dreaming of becoming a horse trainer. And now, six years and one Oscar nomination later, she was about to fly back to the States to shoot her fourth movie. She had top billing, and her publicists were making a big deal to the press about how she did all her own stunts.

No one was especially happy about that last bit because of the insurance, but fuck them. The stunts were the best part. She'd realised pretty quickly the rest of it was tedious, even if she was getting paid a gazillion dollars. And now she was complaining. *Better watch that, Shannon. No one likes an ungrateful movie star.*

"Hey, Shannon?" She turned to face the blonde seated on her left. "Where did you go? You kind of zoned out."

"Nowhere. Just...bored," Shannon replied, waving her hand to indicate the people around her.

"Want to go somewhere else?" Bethany asked.

The two of them had been best friends since high school, and Shannon wanted to surprise Bethany by bringing her to London. She smiled now, remembering Bethany's response when she had called her in Kansas.

The phone had crashed to the ground, and Bethany had squealed at someone in the background, *'Oh my God, I'm going to London!'*

The whole flight over, she'd bugged Shannon, asking if Dane North would be at the premiere. The gossip columns had been trying to link him and Shannon together for months.

In truth, there was nothing was going on at all. Shannon was gay. She didn't think he was, but a public romance between two celebrities sold magazines and raised her profile. She really hated this part of the business, the fakery of it all. Shannon wasn't naïve and knew if she wanted to keep making movies, she needed to play the game. As long as she didn't sell too much of herself in the process, well, that was okay, wasn't it?

Sometimes, she felt guilty about hiding her sexuality. Though she never denied it, she tended to brush off questions about who she was dating or outright refuse to answer them.

Her parents had taught her not to lie, so she didn't—well, not exactly. Although avoidance was pretty much lying when it came down to it. *Wasn't it?* If she worked a regular job, she wouldn't care; she'd tell everyone. Except she didn't work a regular job—she was a *movie star*.

Movie stars didn't tell the world they were gay if they wanted to keep being cast in big-budget productions. Plus, Shannon had a lot of people who relied on her. Not the hangers-on—she didn't give a shit about them—but there was a whole staff she employed who would be out of a job if the golden goose stopped laying. These were people with families and mortgages and car lease agreements.

So, when some nosy reporter asked about a boyfriend and Shannon was tempted to tell the truth, she thought about those people instead and kept her mouth shut, even if she ended up hating herself a little more each time.

"Jesus, Shannon, will you stay on this planet for five minutes?" Bethany tugged on Shannon's arm and rolled her eyes.

"Sorry, Bethy. Where do you want to go?"

Before Bethany could answer, a good-looking guy sat down

"Am I interrupting anything, ladies?" He addressed them both, even though his eyes never left Bethany, and she was already melting under his gaze. Now it was Shannon's turn to roll her eyes.

"No, we were just talking. Come, sit with us." Bethany elbowed Shannon and made her move up the sofa. Shannon shuffled to the end and tuned them out.

While Bethany and Good-Looking Nameless Guy got to know each other, Shannon glanced at her entourage one more time. She was bored, restless. *God, what is wrong with me?* Normally she could cope with the emptiness these evenings made her feel, but right now she was desperate to leave. She wanted to run away and keep on going until she was back on the flat fields of Kansas with the grass tickling her ankles and the sun warming her face.

Back home, her only worry had been making sure she was in time for dinner, and the only consideration she'd had to give to her outfit was taking care not to tear even more holes in her jeans.

Shannon was probably romanticising a little. After all, Kansas was hardly LGBT Headquarters. Even so, she missed it and her town had been more purple than blue or red in its political leanings.

Shannon sighed and stood wearily. She walked to the balcony that overlooked the rest of the bar and stayed for a while to observe all the shiny young pretty things below. She was looking for someone to catch her eye, someone she could lose a few hours with. Shannon wanted a nameless stranger to take away the loneliness and boredom just for a little while. She couldn't run back to Kansas, but she could find a temporary shelter inside one of the women below.

Shannon saw her then, at the bar, leaning back on her stool with the beer bottle in her hand and a moody look on her face. *She's hot.*

Her short dark hair was swept back from her forehead, and her T-shirt rode up just enough to expose a glimpse of tight, muscled belly.

Interesting.

Shannon was no stranger to anonymous hook-ups, and this one might be just the ticket. Resisting her natural urge to go and hunt down the prey herself, she figured she'd better send Claire to pave the way. Another concession she had to make to fame. Like the rest, it didn't sit well with her.

* * *

Jesus, what I am I doing here? Jay spun around on her stool and came face-to-face with a nervous dark-haired woman.

"Hi, I'm Claire." Clearing her throat, Claire extended her hand and waited. Jay watched Claire's hand as it hovered awkwardly between them before she dropped it limply to her side. Jay had no intention of shaking.

"My employer has asked me to come downstairs and invite you to join her for a drink." Claire looked uncomfortable.

"What are you, her pimp? Who's your employer?"

"I'm afraid I can't tell you that. I'll need you to sign a nondisclosure agreement first. My employer is a well-known celebrity."

Claire's voice was tinged with pride, despite the strange situation.

"You're kidding?" Jay smiled humourlessly. "A nondisclosure agreement?"

"Yes—" Claire nodded. "—to prevent any negative press coming to light."

"Listen, love." She leaned forward on the stool, bringing her face close to the other woman and doing her best to be condescending. "I'm not interested, okay?"

Claire flinched. She obviously wasn't used to being told no.

"Maybe you should think about it? My employer—"

"I'm not for sale. It doesn't matter who's paying. Understand?"

Something in her eyes must have convinced Claire. Nodding, she backed away and hurried off.

Jesus, a nondisclosure agreement? Time really does march on. She could remember when you bought someone a drink, made small talk for an hour, then went back to her place. Of course, she'd never had a celebrity want to shag her before. Jay wondered briefly who it might be. *As if you would even know. It's not like you've kept up to date with show business since you've been away.* Even before, when other girls were poring over gossip magazines, she read books about gardening.

Before. That was how she thought of it now. There was *before,* when things had all looked bright and filled with promise, and *now.*

Now was something she didn't really want to dwell on too much.

She nursed the beer for a few minutes longer, unsure why she didn't just leave.

"Hey." A soft American voice roused her from her thoughts. "Did you really call my assistant a pimp?"

The voice alone got her blood up. Husky and low, it had to be the sexiest voice she'd ever heard.

She turned slowly on her stool, taking in the woman before her. Long, wavy, golden-brown hair, and large grey eyes. Surprisingly, Jay knew who she was. Shannon Somebody—she couldn't remember her last name. Jay raked her gaze over the woman's body and lingered purposely on the full, creamy swell of breasts. *Jesus, she is hot.*

* * *

Shannon usually got pissed off when someone blatantly stared at her tits. She wasn't sure why it didn't bother her this time. Even from another woman, it should have. Maybe because the woman ogling her was the same woman who'd just turned her down.

"So, are you going to answer me, or just carrying on fucking me with your eyes?" Shannon asked as she slid onto the barstool beside the woman, pushing her tits out a little more. *That's right. Have a good look at what you just turned down.*

When Claire had come back, flustered and embarrassed, and relayed her conversation with the hot barfly, Shannon hadn't hesitated in marching downstairs. It wasn't often she got turned down—in fact, she couldn't remember it *ever* happening before.

Who the hell does she think she is? Calling my assistant a pimp? Shannon caught herself at the bottom of the stairs. The woman was still on her stool looking moodily around the room with a slight air of bored arrogance which, to her surprise, Shannon found appealing. She felt the familiar tingle between her legs and decided maybe this prey would be worth chasing.

"Drink?" the woman asked, ignoring Shannon's eye-fucking comment with a half-smile on her full lips.

"Honey, my drink costs eighty pounds a glass," Shannon replied. She leaned forward and offered another view of her chest. To the woman's credit, this time her eyes didn't leave Shannon's face.

"Fuck that then. You can buy *me* drink."

Shannon frowned. She didn't know what to say because this never happened either. The woman broke into a smile, and it was like the clouds had parted—she looked even sexier when she smiled.

Shannon grinned in return.

"You have a name?" Shannon asked. She switched back effortlessly to seductress. And she was definitely dressed for seduction. Tight black dress that dipped low, but tastefully, to allow a good view of her cleavage. The dress came up short at the bottom, exposing creamy thighs and long, shapely legs. Like an animal on the hunt, Shannon gave herself the best possible advantage every time. And now the other woman's eyes were back on her cleavage.

"Jesus, will you stop eye-fucking me for one second and tell me your name?"

"Jay." The woman dragged her eyes back up to Shannon's face.

"Short for Jayne?" Shannon asked.

"No, short for Jay."

"I see. What are you drinking?" She reached out to the bottle, running her finger down the length of it, and noticed Jay squirm a little on her seat.

"Beer," she replied, and Shannon saw her throat work to swallow. *Dry mouth. Good.*

"Hm." She let her finger continue downwards to brush Jay's hand. "Let's get another round of these."

Jay signalled the barman and ordered two more bottles. "So, don't you want to know my name?" Shannon asked.

"I know who you are," Jay answered quietly as she watched Shannon hand over money to the barman.

"Well, that's refreshing."

"Why?" Jay took a long pull on her beer. Her eyes never left Shannon's. A little of it escaped her lips and began to run down her mouth, to the side of her jaw. Shannon reached out her thumb and wiped away the drip, then sucked it off.

Jay laughed. "You are such a cliché. Turn-Ons 101."

"Is it working?" Shannon smiled.

"Beautifully." Jay replied ruefully. "Kind of wish I'd signed that nondisclosure thing now."

"Yep, you should have." Shannon sighed. "I'm not supposed to screw anyone without it." She leaned forward again and discreetly stroked the inside of Jay's thigh, pleased when the muscles clenched. "For you, I might make an exception."

"Pretty decent of you." Jay's voice was strained and a little raw.

"Uh-huh," Shannon leaned back, climbed down from her stool. "Wait here. I need to get my stuff."

"Just like that?"

"What do you mean?" Shannon reached over and drained her beer.

"You don't even know me."

"That's kind of the point, honey." Shannon regarded Jay steadily, noting she looked uncertain. "Second thoughts?"

"I'm not sure."

"Look—" Shannon blew out a breath. "I'm looking for a good time. If that's not your thing, let me know and I'll move on."

"Just like that?" Jay drained her own beer, eyes never leaving Shannon's.

"In or out?" Unsure why, Shannon was really hoping she would say she was in.

"Go and get your stuff." Jay inclined her head towards the balcony above.

"Sure?"

Jay nodded.

* * *

Bethany was still in deep conversation with Nameless Guy when she'd gone back upstairs. It took her a few moments to get Bethany's attention, and when she looked up at Shannon, she had a dreamy look in her eyes. Shannon wanted to hug her she was so sweet.

She told Bethany she was going back to the hotel because she wasn't feeling well. Bethany's eyes narrowed.

"You liar. What's going on?"

"Nothing's going on."

"Sure it isn't."

Shannon sighed. She could never keep anything from her best friend. For all her innocence Bethany was a damn bloodhound. "I met someone downstairs. There, are you happy now?"

"I haven't decided. What's her name?"

"Why is that important? It's only for tonight."

"Well, if she strangles you and chops you into tiny pieces, at least I'll have a name for the police."

Shannon rolled her eyes. "Bethy, I'll be fine. Don't worry about me. Will you be okay here?"

"Sure, I'll have Mark take me back to the hotel."

"Are you sure, Bethy? I don't want to leave you with a stranger."

Bethany snorted. "Says you, about to head off into the sunset with a hook-up. I'm fine. Really. Go, get laid. With luck, I might be joining you." At Shannon's raised eyebrow, Bethany blushed. "Not like that! Jesus! With Mark."

"I know. I'm kidding. Be safe. You have my cell. Need any cash?"

"No! Shannon, don't worry. *Go.*"

* * *

They sat side by side in the black cab, not touching, but Shannon could feel the heat pouring off Jay.

Shannon felt reckless. She'd picked up strangers for sex before, so she didn't know why it felt different this time. Maybe because she didn't have a nondisclosure agreement. Her publicists would kill her.

Jay paid the cab driver, waving away Shannon's offer of money. She liked that. She was used to being the one who paid.

* * *

Jay was having trouble—real trouble—keeping her hands to herself. When two more people got into the lift, she was forced to stand closer to Shannon. She groaned inwardly. She couldn't get to the hotel room fast enough. Jay could smell Shannon's perfume, light and sweet. She was already imagining those full, creamy tits in her hands and Shannon's long legs wrapped around her.

Jay had let Shannon walk into the lift before her and got a great view of her arse. It twitched from side to side as she walked, and it was firm and round—the perfect size. Most of the actresses she'd seen on DVDs in the TV room were skinny. Shannon was slim, but curvy in all the right places. Jay groaned again and caught Shannon's self-satisfied grin.

Finally, they were here. Shannon swiped her card and ushered Jay into a suite that was as big as any flat Jay had ever seen. She whistled, lust momentarily forgotten.

"You like it?" Shannon asked, stepping out of her heels which made her about four inches shorter than Jay.

"Yes, it's nice." Jay walked to the floor-to-ceiling windows which gave a spectacular view of Hyde Park.

"Cool view, huh?" Shannon stepped up close behind her, not touching. Jay could feel warm breath on her neck and smell her perfume which she knew she would always associate with Shannon from now on. Jay swallowed hard at the sudden rush of heat between her legs.

"You want a drink?" Shannon leaned closer still, her lips just brushing Jay's ear, making her shiver.

"No," she said hoarsely. When Jay turned around, their faces where inches apart.

"What *do* you want?" Shannon asked quietly.

"This," Jay whispered. She touched her lips to Shannon's and closed her eyes.

She heard Shannon sigh as her hands came up to rest on Jay's shoulders. Shannon pulled her in and deepened the kiss as she captured Jay's tongue and sucked on it.

Overwhelmed by sensation, Jay's last thread of self-control snapped. She reached up and tugged the zip on Shannon's dress down her back, slid the dress from her shoulders, and let it fall to the ground. Shannon stepped out of it.

Jay turned her in her arms and pushed her against the full-length window, then dropped to her knees. She dragged down Shannon's lacy knickers, and Shannon kicked out of them, moaning softly as Jay's hands came around her and held her firmly in place.

Jay felt Shannon's hands in her hair, gripping it tight in her fists and tugging. The feeling was somewhere between pleasure and pain. Shannon pulled Jay's head back and away from her.

"What?" Jay asked impatiently.

"I like it rough, so no fucking around with nibbles and kisses," Shannon demanded.

She released Jay's head and leaned back against the glass.

"Hurry up. I want to come."

Jay laughed, turned on even more by Shannon's commands. *If that's how she wants to play.*

Jay pushed Shannon's legs apart roughly and used her fingers to spread her wide open. Shannon was swollen and wet, and Jay breathed in the scent of her.

Shannon gasped as Jay's hot mouth closed on her. She shut her eyes and pressed back harder into the wall, pulling Jay's face with her.

She sighed as Jay stroked her tongue rhythmically against Shannon's clit. Jay's mouth was hot and her tongue hard, exactly the way she liked it. Jay unerringly found the spot that would make Shannon come and made circles over it with her tongue.

Her fingers found Shannon's wet and swollen opening, and she pushed inside without hesitation. Jay's arm came around Shannon's waist to hold her in place. With firm strokes, she began to fuck her in a way that Shannon knew would make her come hard. Shannon steadied herself by gripping Jay's firm shoulders and felt her climax began to build, spurred on by the sounds of Jay's groans as she worked her with her tongue and hand.

Hot white heat eclipsed her vision as a fire kindled and caught in her belly. The flames shot up then went raging through her. She cried out, coming forcefully as her legs gave way completely.

Jay caught her, lifted her, and in complete contrast to way she just fucked her, placed Shannon gently on the bed. With infinite tenderness Jay kissed her on her forehead, her eyelids, her chin. Shannon heard her kick off her own shoes and lay down next to her.

"Jesus." Shannon rolled onto her side to face Jay. "That was unexpected."

"What do you mean?" Jay turned her head to face Shannon.

"Usually I have a little wine and make conversation first. But you just dove straight in there—not that I'm complaining."

Shannon ran her hand down Jay's stomach. She lifted her T-shirt and drew slow circles at the base of her belly. She was pleased when she felt the muscles twitch and tighten.

"I just noticed I'm the only one of us that's naked," Shannon said.

Jay grinned and reached up to stroke Shannon's face. She trailed her fingers down her neck before gently capturing a small pink nipple. Shannon gasped. She wasn't ready to come again, and she needed to touch Jay.

Shannon took the hand from her breast, pushed it back above Jay's head, and then did the same with the other.

She rolled over and came to rest on top of Jay, still holding her arms in place. Shannon pushed one leg between Jay's and began to move slowly back and forth so the seam of Jay's jeans pressed against her clit.

Jay raised her head to suck on one of Shannon's full breasts as they swayed above her. "No." Shannon moved away and then ducked her head quickly, nipping Jay's chin.

"You're the boss," Jay breathed.

"I am. And don't you forget it," Shannon murmured, releasing her arms and reaching down to unzip Jay's jeans. She slid a hand inside to find Jay wet and ready for her.

Shannon kissed Jay deeply and swallowed her gasp as she brushed gentle fingers over her clit.

"You like that?" Shannon crooned, running a finger up and then back down the cleft of Jay's lips.

"Yes." Jay groaned. "I'm going to come."

"No you're not. Not until I say you can." Shannon removed her hand, tugged Jay's jeans down her legs, and threw them behind her. She pulled up her T-shirt, and Jay helped her get it off. Now, both naked, Shannon slid down Jay's hard, slick body and rested between her legs.

She pressed her thumb to Jay's wet centre and tugged lightly, drawing a soft groan. She smiled, dropped her head, and licked slowly along the length of Jay's clit, then drew it into her mouth and sucked. Jay bucked on the bed, moaning softly.

"That feel good?" Shannon asked, lifting her head.

"Yes, fuck yes." Jay's eyes were squeezed shut. "Please, don't stop."

Shannon's head dipped again as she pulled Jay's hard, swollen clit between her lips. She sucked steadily, and Jay's hips rocked in time, becoming more frantic with every stroke, until, finally, she held Shannon's head to her, her body going rigid for a moment, and then lay still.

Shannon looked up. Jay was still with one arm flung across her eyes. She moved up on the bed and pulled her arm away.

"Did you come?" she asked.

Jay nodded her head, eyes still closed.

"You're very quiet. Maybe we need to work out a hand signal or something."

Jay didn't respond.

"What's the matter? Hit your word limit for the day?" Shannon slapped her belly softly, then lay beside her.

"I haven't been with anyone for a really long time," Jay finally said, her voice quiet.

"How long?" Shannon turned on her side, one hand supporting her head.

"Five years."

"You're kidding me?"

"No, I'm not."

Jay finally opened her eyes, and Shannon was surprised at the pain in them. She reached out and stroked Jay's face gently—something she never did because it was so intimate—but the woman looked so damn sad.

"Why? I mean, you're really sexy."

"Thanks." Jay grinned. "Let me show you just how sexy."

She began to rise. Shannon pushed her back down firmly. "Not so fast, hot stuff. Tell me."

Jay blew out a breath. "I've been away."

"Where? A convent?"

Jay sat up, then pushed a hand through her hair. "Are you always this nosy?"

"Pretty much," Shannon answered.

"I've been inside," Jay replied, slowly.

Shannon didn't understand. "Like agoraphobia?"

"No." Jay laughed, then grew serious. "Like prison."

It took a moment to sink in.

"Prison," Shannon repeated. *Oh shit. The one time I don't get a nondisclosure agreement.*

"Yes. Five years." Jay must have seen the look of panic on Shannon's face because she began to move off the bed.

"Hey, where are you going?" Shannon stilled her with an arm.

"You can't want me to stay after I just told you that."

"I don't know," Shannon said honestly. "What did you do?" *Shannon, it doesn't matter what she did. This is so not good for your career.* The truth was that she really didn't want her to go.

Remembering the way Jay had lain her on the bed so carefully, Shannon couldn't believe Jay meant her any harm. *You don't know that.* Except somehow she did. And besides, Jay had plenty of opportunity to strangle her and chop her into tiny pieces—like Bethany was worried about.

"Does it matter?" Jay sat on the edge of the bed, facing the window, breaking Shannon from her internal struggle.

Shannon sat up behind her and ran her hand over the tattoo on her neck, a crudely drawn constellation—maybe the Little Dipper—and no doubt something she'd picked up in prison.

"You're safe with me, Shannon. I wouldn't hurt you," Jay said quietly as she began to relax beneath Shannon's gentle touch.

"I know," Shannon replied. Her hand moved up into Jay's hair and stroked softly. "Don't go. Please."

Jay was surprised. She fully expected Shannon to kick her out after what she'd told her.

Jay turned back towards the bed and into Shannon's outstretched arms. She pushed her gently back down on the bed and kissed her softly, surprising herself with her own tenderness.

With her fingers, she traced the line of Shannon's jaw, then her lips, and then kissed the places she had touched. Shannon sighed and arched her neck to allow Jay easier access.

Slowly, Jay worked her way down to Shannon's breasts, drew circles around her nipple, and watched as it hardened. She flicked her tongue over it, and Shannon gasped at the sensation. Jay took the nipple in her mouth and sucked, while she rolled the other one between her fingers. She slid her leg between Shannon's and groaned softly as she felt wetness against her thigh.

Shannon lifted her head up and covered Jay's mouth with her own. Shannon pulled her down and locked her ankle around Jay's calf as she rocked against her leg. She forced her thigh against Jay's wet, warm centre, and they both began to move frantically. Jay braced herself on her arms and squeezed her eyes shut.

She felt Shannon grasp her head between her hands.

"Look at me," she gasped. "Look...at...me."

Jay opened her eyes and tried to stay focused on Shannon as she rocked above her, climbing steadily to orgasm.

Eyes locked, they rode the wave together, Shannon cried out while Jay remained silent. She lowered herself into Shannon's arms and buried her face in her neck for a moment, then tried to roll away.

"No, stay." Shannon held her in place.

At first it felt uncomfortable to be held like that, then she relaxed into it. Shannon stroked her back, finding the tattoo on her neck, running her fingers over the ridged bumps.

* * *

Shannon finally felt content. Her limbs were liquid, and the tension from earlier in the evening had completely dissipated. She traced the outline of Jay's tattoo, a delicate scar on soft smooth skin. She wanted to ask what it was for, but didn't.

Her parents had a horse farm back in Kansas. Sometimes, she'd watched her father break the horses in. When she was older, he'd let her help, and she'd been good at it. The trick was patience. Going too fast or too hard would spook them. Like any animal, they didn't trust easily; it took time. When they were ready, when they learned you weren't going to hurt them, they came around.

In her arms, Jay spoke against her neck. "You didn't answer my question earlier." She rolled onto her back, folding her hands behind her head.

Shannon turned on her side to face Jay. "What do you mean?"

"When I said I already knew your name. You said it was refreshing. What did you mean?"

"Oh, that. Usually when I meet people, it goes one of two ways. They either fawn all over me or pretend they don't know who I am. Whichever way they go, it ends up the same way. *I'm an actress, you know. I've got this screenplay I wrote.* You get the picture." Shannon waved her hand dismissively. "You didn't do any of that. It's nice."

"Really?" Jay turned to face her. "You know, I'm an actress..." She grinned.

"Fuck off." Shannon laughed and slapped her chest lightly. "Have you ever seen one of my movies?"

"Yes, one. Can't remember what it was called though. It was all right."

"*All right*?" Shannon mimicked Jay's accent. "Just *all right*?"

"I'm not into those romantic ones. But that's all we got in prison. Romantic comedies. I suppose they worried that anything a bit grittier, and we'd get all worked up and start stabbing each other or something."

"I've never been in a romantic comedy." Shannon sat up, annoyed.

"Yes you have. That one where you have to go back to high school undercover. You end up with the teacher."

"I never did a movie like that. *Ever.*"

"Are you sure?" Jay asked.

"I know what fucking movies I've been in," Shannon snapped.

"Must have been some other bird then." Jay shrugged and yawned.

"*Some other bird*? Are you serious? You know... Wait... Are you...?" Shannon stopped as Jay began to laugh.

"Oh, you fucker!" Shannon threw a pillow at her.

Jay caught it and carried on laughing. "Sorry, I couldn't help it."

Shannon couldn't stop herself from smiling. This, she wasn't used to. When she'd been back in Kansas, people had joked around with her, but since she became a movie star, no one dared. They were all too busy kissing her ass. She didn't realise how much she missed being treated like a normal human being. "You're an asshole," she said as she lay back down and stretched out alongside Jay. "You're lucky that you're good in bed."

"It's sexy when you swear in that accent." Jay rolled over to face her, her hand trailing over Shannon's hip to rest on her backside. "You want to go again?"

"When you it put so romantically, how could I refuse?" Shannon rolled onto her and pushed her back into the bed. "This time, I'm in charge."

"Whatever you want." Jay's eyes darkened as Shannon rose up to straddle her. "I want you to watch me," Shannon told her as she teased her own nipples to attention and rocked against Jay's belly.

"Okay," Jay breathed.

"And no touching until I say so."

"Okay."

"Good."

Shannon reached down and began to stroke herself. Distantly, she heard Jay groan.

"You like watching me?" She breathed, feeling herself swell and get wet.

"Oh yes," Jay whispered as her hands twitched by her sides.

Shannon began stroke herself harder before she pushed one, two fingers inside herself and groaned. She pulled them back out and ran them over Jay's lips, before pushing them into Jay's mouth. Jay's head rose up as she sucked on Shannon's fingers, tasting her sweetness.

"You want to be inside me, baby?" Shannon crooned, her hand going back to pleasuring herself.

"Can I?" Jay croaked, her throat tight and dry.

"Not yet. Not just yet." Shannon stroked herself faster, harder, rocking her hips in time. "I'm going to come," she moaned as she felt the tide of her orgasm rise.

"Jesus." Jay groaned.

"Now, Jay, go inside," Shannon commanded, and Jay complied.

Shannon felt Jay's gentle fingers push inside, and she groaned. Her building orgasm receded slightly until Jay picked up the same rhythm she'd used on herself.

Jay slipped out and then pushed back inside again. Shannon began to rock harder, and Jay held her hand in place, letting Shannon ride her fingers.

Shannon picked up her pace until she was hammering up and down frantically. She threw her head back and cried out, collapsing into Jay's waiting arms.

* * *

Shannon had fallen asleep in her arms, and though Jay was tired herself, she couldn't sleep. Maybe it was the unusual sensation of someone else in the bed with her. Or maybe the fact that she lay beneath soft warm sheets instead of on a hard, lumpy mattress. She wasn't sure, but it felt good. So she lay there and ran her fingers through Shannon's thick, golden-brown hair.

When she'd stepped out of the prison gates that morning, a hotel was the last place she'd expected to end up. She'd gone to the crappy boarding house where she'd rented a crappy room through the prison service reintegration programme.

She sat down on a bed, which dipped heavily in the middle, and tried not to think of all the other sweating bodies that had lain on it before her. She tried to get her head straight.

She'd taken three worn paperbacks out of her duffle bag and put them on the window sill, moved her small collection of clothes into the chest of drawers which was scarred with cigarette burns, and wondered how the fuck she'd ended up here. Not the boarding house—that place was where they sent recent parolees. She'd known for ages she'd be starting again there. How had she ended up *here*? In the mess she'd found herself in?

She had a job interview next week at a supermarket. Another shithole that employed paroled prisoners for minimum wage. When she'd told her prison liaison officer there was no way she was working in a supermarket, the woman had given her a cold hard look. *"For next few months, you'll be out on license. You mess up once—just once—and you'll be straight back here. Someone like you, Jay, doesn't have many choices. So take the room in the boarding house, go to work at the supermarket, and be grateful that you're out. That you're free. Try and make some kind of life for yourself. Even if it isn't what you had planned."*

She'd been good in school and about to start a degree in agriculture at university. She'd had friends, been on the hockey team. Then it had all gone spectacularly wrong.

She sighed and rubbed her grainy eyes.

Shannon stirred. "What's wrong?" she asked sleepily.

"Nothing. Go back to sleep," Jay whispered and kissed her hair.

Shannon rose up onto her side and yawned. "Aren't you tired?" she asked.

"Yes, but I can't seem to go to sleep."

"Seriously? After what we've been doing? Sex doesn't put you to sleep?"

Jay shrugged.

Shannon sighed. "Come here." She rolled onto her back and held out her arms. Without thinking, Jay moved into them, and Shannon directed her head to her chest and stroked her hair.

"You don't have to do this," Jay mumbled.

"I know, but the alternative is you lying there all night, fidgeting."

"I can go," she said, hoping desperately that Shannon wouldn't let her, and not knowing why she felt like that.

"I'd rather you didn't," Shannon replied softly.

"Okay then. I won't."

"Good."

Shannon felt Jay relax and go heavy in her arms as she fell asleep. Shannon lay there for a while, wondering about Jay and what the fuck she, Shannon, was doing.

She'd invited women to her bed before, women she didn't know—didn't want to know. She was always glad when they left, ushering them out of the door when she'd had enough, and she never let them stay the night. *Ever.*

Now here she was, lying in bed with a former criminal asleep in her arms, and wanting desperately to know her. To heal her. *Fuck. What am I doing?* And she hadn't even gotten her to sign the nondisclosure agreement. Somehow and for reasons she didn't understand, Shannon trusted Jay. Jay would never say a word to anyone. Shannon didn't know how she knew, but it was true.

She knew, just like she had known how far to push the horses. An instinct that told her when they were ready to be mounted, when they wouldn't throw her off and hurt her. Sighing, she pulled Jay tighter and slept.

* * *

Shannon woke to the sound of shrill ringing. She reached across the still-sleeping body of Jay and grabbed her cell phone.

"Yes?" Her voice was still thick with sleep.

"Shannon? Did I wake you up?"

Shannon sat up. "Yes, what time is it?"

"Like, after ten. Guess you're worn out from last night, huh?" Bethany teased.

"A little bit." Shannon glanced down at Jay, who lay on her back, arms above her head with the sheet pushed down to just below her waist. Something stirred in Shannon again.

"What's up?" She forced her mind back the Bethany.

"Oh, nothing. Did we have plans today?"

"Are you with that guy?"

"Mark. Yes, he wants to take me out for the day. Show me the sights, he says."

Hmmm, maybe Nameless Guy wasn't such a douchebag after all. "And you want to go?"

"Do you mind?" Bethany sounded hesitant. "I mean, I know this was supposed to be time for us to hang out and, you know, catch up and stuff."

"Bethy, it's fine. Seriously, enjoy yourself."

"Really? Are you sure?"

"I'm sure."

"Wait a minute, is she still there?"

Shannon could hear sheets rustling on the other end of the line. She smiled, imagining Bethany sitting up, eyes bright and nose twitching with the scent of gossip.

When Shannon didn't reply, Bethany put two and two together. "*Oh my God*, she stayed over?"

"Bethy—"

"Well, well, well. Shannon Dempsey. Did this one get under your skin?"

"Bethy." Shannon squirmed. "I can't talk about it right now. I'll see you tomorrow? The car's taking us to the airport at eight."

"Sure. But as your best friend, I want all the details. *All* of them."

"Fine, fine. Now get lost and enjoy your day with lover boy."

Bethany suddenly squealed on the other end of the line, and Shannon heard a quiet male voice. "Okay, Shannon, I gotta go. Love you."

"Love you, Bethy." Shannon ended the call and smiled. She looked back at Jay, who was now watching her with those sexy, hooded eyes. Her hands were folded behind her head.

"Hey," Jay said softly.

"Hey, yourself." Shannon lay down alongside her and ran her hands in slow circles on Jay's belly.

"Who was that?"

"My friend, Bethany. She hooked up with a guy last night." Shannon trailed one finger down Jay's abdomen, stopping just below her navel. She smiled at Jay's quick intake of breath. "She wants to hang out with him today. He's going to show her the sights."

"I see." Jay's voice was tight with arousal. "And what are your plans today?" Jay caught her hand as it began a slow descent past her navel.

"I thought unless you had stuff to do, you could show me your sights. If you do, I'll show you mine."

Shannon met her eyes and grinned at Jay. Seeing a serious look returned, she wasn't sure what it meant. "What?" Shannon frowned, uncertain.

"It's just...you're so beautiful." Jay rose, caught Shannon's face in her hand, and gently ran her thumb over her jaw. She kissed her softly, a lover's kiss.

Shannon closed her eyes, allowing herself, for a moment, to believe that this was her lover, not just some random woman she had picked up at a bar. Jay slowly deepened the kiss, rolling over until she was on top of Shannon.

Jay kissed her way along Shannon's jaw and down her neck. She took a nipple in her mouth and began to suck it gently while her hand travelled downwards, stroking, stroking, carefully, slowly.

Shannon arched beneath her and couldn't help herself from running her hands through the thick, soft hair on Jay's head. She sighed as Jay placed gentle kisses on the inside of her thighs. Jay smiled against her skin when she couldn't contain her moan.

Jay trailed her fingers lightly on Shannon's outer lips, then took one gently in her mouth and sucked. When Shannon groaned again, Jay stopped and moved onto the other one. Jay opened her with infinite care and then run her tongue along the length of her clit.

"Wait, wait, stop," Shannon said.

It was too much. Too much like making love and it had to stop.

"Did I do something wrong?" Jay's head came up, her eyes worried.

"No, baby, no." Shannon reached down to stroke her face. "Just turn around, I want to taste you too."

She did; it wasn't a lie, but it wasn't quite the truth either. She couldn't let Jay make love to her. Her heart would break.

Shannon had spent such a long time learning to protect herself, walling herself off from everyone except Bethany and her family. One gentle touch, one caress from Jay, and she could feel it all being swept away like a child's building blocks. What was wrong with her that this one woman she hardly knew could render her so vulnerable?

Jay did as she was asked and rose up quickly. She turned and placed her arms and legs either side of Shannon, her centre hovered above Shannon's mouth.

Shannon closed her eyes and concentrated on the scent of Jay, on the taste of her. She reminded herself it was just sex.

* * *

Shannon rolled away and lay on her back as she tried to catch her breath. Jay reached for her hand.

"Wow," Shannon managed.

"I know," Jay replied.

"Give me a minute and I'll order some breakfast."

"I'm starving." Jay turned over and used her finger to trace the valley between Shannon's breasts.

"No fucking way." Shannon shoved her hand away. "You can't want to go again."

Jay grinned. "Five years is a long time, you know."

"You were in a women's prison. You couldn't have got yourself off with anyone?"

Jay rolled away and sat up. "No. I'm going to make some tea."

"Hey," Shannon said softly, holding Jay's arm as she went to move away. "Sorry, it was a stupid joke."

"It's okay, you don't need to apologise," Jay said.

"I do. I shouldn't have made a joke about prison. Sometimes, I'm an idiot."

Jay rolled back onto the bed, planting a loud kiss on her breast. "Nah, you're not an idiot."

She tickled Shannon ribs and made her squeal.

"Get lost!" She laughed, slapping at Jay's hands.

"Oh, the movie star's ticklish," Jay said, reaching for her.

"I mean it, get lost!" Shannon squealed again as Jay caught her. She wriggled free and jumped from the bed, laughing. "Asshole."

"I love it when you call me names in American," Jay joked and got up to join her. "You want tea?" She turned over two mugs at the marble-top counter.

"Sure, I'll order up some breakfast. What do you eat?"

"Full English." Jay didn't turn around. She was focussed on the tea making.

"That sounds disgusting. What is it?" Shannon picked up the menu and began reading. "Meat, meat, meat, and baked beans?"

"It's lovely. Have one."

"I'll pass, thanks."

"I suppose you Hollywood lot mostly eat, what, dust?" Jay brought the mugs over to the bed and placed one of them on Shannon's side.

"Not me. I mean, I have to exercise, but I don't starve myself."

"No, I can see that," Jay said, drawing her eyes down Shannon's body.

"Take a picture, it'll last longer." Shannon rolled her eyes, even though she liked the way Jay looked at her.

"Oh yes, your nondisclosure people would love that."

"They'd have a coronary."

"So, what, you're gay, but you pretend to be straight?" Jay asked, with no judgement in her voice.

Shannon looked at her as she sipped her tea. "I avoid the subject. Lie by omission, I guess. I mean, some actors do come out, but if you want to get the good parts—especially as a woman—you need to be seen as fuckable, attainable. A lesbian is none of those things to the men who make or watch movies." She shrugged. There was no anger in her voice.

"That's unfair. I mean, isn't the point of acting that you're acting? You're being someone else?"

"It's just the way it is. It's changing slowly, but for right now, I let everyone assume I'm straight. When the rumour mill churns about me and some guy dating, I don't deny or confirm it. The current one is that I'm dating my co-star, Dane North."

"Who?" Jay asked, puzzled.

"That's why I like you, Jay. You really don't give a shit, do you?" Shannon laughed and picked the menu up again. "Let's get this food ordered. I'm so hungry."

* * *

"That's the best meal I've had in ages." Jay leaned back in her chair at the dining table. They had moved to the other end of the suite and were now showered and dressed. Shannon wore loose cotton trousers and a vest. Jay decided she liked her better this way. Her face was scrubbed clean of makeup, and her wet hair was starting to dry in long waves around her shoulders.

"Was the food bad in—sorry." Shannon stopped herself.

"It's fine. You can ask about it. Yes, the food was bad in prison—like school dinners."

"School what?"

"You know, the food you get at lunchtime in school."

"Oh yes, I remember that. Gross. Was it... Did you... I mean, can I ask, was it horrible in there?" Shannon asked nervously, not wanting to spook her.

Jay studied Shannon for a moment, unsure how much she wanted to say. She decided there was nothing more than curiosity behind Shannon's question. "No. It wasn't that bad, really. I mean, once you got used to the fact that you couldn't go outside whenever you wanted. Or that you had no personal freedom. It was okay."

"Seriously?"

"Yes. I mean, don't get me wrong, I don't want to go back. At first, it was really hard. I got into a few scrapes at first, people trying it on—"

"Trying to rape you?" Shannon was horrified.

"No! Not that. Just trying to take my food, or my stuff, trying to rough me up—I was only eighteen at the time. They thought I was an easy touch."

Jay was only eighteen when she was put in prison. The age Shannon was now and she couldn't imagine being locked away for five years like that. Time passing you by outside, going in a teenager and coming out at twenty-three.

"You aren't angry about it?" Shannon asked.

"Being locked up? No, I committed a crime, and I deserved to be punished for it. I'm not angry or resentful. Being in prison is one of the things I'm not angry about." A shadow passed over her face, and Shannon reached across the table to take her hand.

"What are you angry about?" she asked softly, not understanding why she needed to know this woman like she did.

"Lots of things," Jay answered, just as softly. "It doesn't matter now."

"Do you have family?" Shannon asked.

"Yes, a mother and a sister, but they won't speak to me anymore."

Shannon saw the pain etched deep in her face. She stood, walked around the table, and then deposited herself in Jay's lap. "I'm sorry," she whispered, stroking her head.

Jay leaned into her for a moment, accepting the comfort.

"Thanks," Jay replied and leaned back. "Anyway, I've told you all this stuff about me. What about you?"

"What about me?" Shannon asked, feeling defensive. It was her default response to personal questions. Her lessons in trust had been hard ones. The evidence of a misplaced word or conversation splattered across the tabloids and gossip magazines. She'd learned deflection, learned to censor her words so that nothing out of her mouth was anything other than what she wanted people to know.

Jay must have sensed her discomfort at the personal question. "I'm sorry, I didn't mean to pry. You don't have to tell me anything."

"No, it's okay. I don't mind," Shannon surprised herself by answering. "I guess I'm just wary these days. What did you want to know?"

After everything Jay had told her, she didn't see any harm in reciprocating. Besides, she trusted Jay. It made no sense when she'd only met her last night, but she knew Jay would never sell her out.

"Where are you from?"

"Kansas. Heard of it?" Shannon moved from her lap and took a seat beside her.

"Yes. *Wizard of Oz.*"

"Right." Shannon laughed.

"You like it there?" Jay asked.

"Sure. I mean, it's flat, and there isn't a whole lot going on, but I love it. My family has a horse farm. It's nothing fancy, but it does all right."

"You're close with them?" Jay asked again.

Shannon was surprised to discover talking about her family didn't make her uncomfortable as it usually did. Perhaps because she sensed no ulterior motive behind Jay's interest.

"Yes, we talk all the time, and I get back whenever I can." Shannon saw a shadow pass over Jay's face again and wondered about this lost woman. "I have five brothers," she said.

"*What?* That must have been fun growing up."

"Actually, it was. All that space, freedom. Nobody cared who I was back then, and I could just be me."

Shannon was surprised when Jay took her hand.

"Does your family know about you being gay?" Jay asked gently.

"Yes, and they're thoroughly disappointed in me."

"For being gay?" Jay looked shocked.

"No, for being in the closet. They don't care at all about my being gay. They're wonderful people," Shannon said wistfully. "I think they wish I'd stayed on the farm. I was good with the horses."

"Are the rest of your family still there?" Jay asked.

"One of my brothers went to Kansas City. He's a lawyer now. The others are still there. All except one—the one above me—is married with kids."

"You're the youngest?"

"Yes, my dad wanted to keep trying until they got a girl."

"You're close to your dad then?"

"I'm close to my mom too, but me and my dad, we both love the horses, you know?" Shannon picked a square of melon from her plate and popped it into her mouth.

Jay didn't understand why she was so interested in Shannon's life. For some reason, she wanted to know everything about her—was greedy for information. Shannon fascinated her, and not in a celebrity way. Jay couldn't care less about that. Shannon did something to her that made her feel a little less hopeless and a little less lost.

"What happened to your dad?" Shannon asked Jay.

"He died when I was four. My mum was pregnant with my sister."

"I'm sorry."

"Don't be. It was a long time ago."

"You were close?" Jay thought about Shannon's question for a moment. Her memories of her father were hazy. A big man, lifting her onto his shoulders, her small hands fisted in his dark, curly hair. Being swung around in strong arms, her screeching with delight. Being held, staring up at the stars. *'Daddy, where do they all come from?'*

'They come from space, darling. They're huge explosions in the sky.'

"I think so. My memories are pretty hazy, but I remember I loved him." Jay shrugged and stood. She didn't want to talk about her father. It hurt too much and inevitably led her down a path of wondering how different things might be if he'd lived.

* * *

They spent most of the day in bed. By the time they came up for air, the sun was setting, and it cast a warm yellow glow over the bed.

Jay propped herself up. She pushed pillows behind her and pulled Shannon's head to her chest. Together, they watched the sun disappear and shadows stretch out inside the hotel suite.

"Will you stay tonight? My car doesn't come for me until tomorrow morning," Shannon asked softly as Jay ran fingers through her hair, fanning the strands onto her chest.

"I'd like that," she replied.

"Good." Shannon didn't understand the sadness inside herself. *It couldn't be because of Jay, could it?* They'd only known each other a day, so she couldn't be sad about leaving her. That wasn't how things worked. To take her mind off the ache inside, she lifted her head, taking one of Jay's small, pink nipples in her mouth. She sucked hard, satisfied when she heard Jay hiss a breath through her teeth. Her hand drifted down between Jay's legs, and she lazily drew circles around her clit.

"Shan...babe...I don't think I can," Jay said in a strangled voice.

Shannon looked at her, one eyebrow raised. "That's not what your body is saying."

"My body doesn't know what it's talking about. I'm really sore— everywhere. I need a break—can't believe I'm actually saying that."

"How about if, this time, I do the work?" Shannon rose up on her knees, watching a lazy smile form on Jay's face.

"That might be okay."

"Thought that might appeal to you. Lay down," she ordered.

Jay complied, and Shannon sat on her at a slight diagonal with one leg over Jay's and the other bent beneath Jay, so their sexes met. Shannon groaned softly and moved her hips in slow circles. She reached down and opened herself. With the other hand she did the same to Jay and brought them together at their centres.

Jay's arms came up, around her waist, holding her down firmly, dictating the pace as she rocked her hips against her.

"Yes, that's it," Shannon groaned and felt her wetness mingle with Jay's. She slid back and forth over her.

She watched as Jay's breathing became laboured, and her eyes squeezed shut as she began to rock in time.

"No, Jay. Look at me. I want you to watch me come."

Jay's eyes opened, and her hands left Shannon's hips as she reached up, fingers closing over Shannon's nipples. She began to manipulate them gently.

"Oh!" Shannon cried out. "I'm coming."

The wave washed over her, and distantly she heard Jay groan. Shannon struggled to continue her rocking motion. She wanted Jay to come as well.

"Are you coming?" she asked, breathlessly.

"Yes," Jay sighed.

"Then...let me...hear you—oh God, I'm coming again."

Shannon groaned. Her eyes flew open as she heard Jay cry out—a hoarse shout of triumph—and she collapsed onto her. Jay wrapped her in her arms and pulled her close. With her head against Jay's neck, she sighed as Jay's hands gently rubbed small circles on her back. Shannon drifted into sleep.

* * *

Jay woke up to the sound of quiet murmurs which came from the dining area. She groaned, pulled herself into a sitting position, and squinted against the bright sunlight coming through the floor-to-ceiling windows.

Her body was sore—pleasantly so—and she grinned at the memories of last night. Fast on the heels of that was the realisation Shannon was flying home today, and the grin dropped off her face.

Although they'd only spent a short amount of time together, most of it fucking, she liked Shannon. Jay couldn't remember the last time she'd met anybody she liked.

Shannon was beautiful and sexy, but Jay had been surprised to discover she was also funny and gentle and kind. *No point getting all mushy about her.* In a few hours, she'd be gone back to America and Jay would probably never see her again.

She sighed and stretched, suddenly noticing the feeling of soft cotton sheets and a firm mattress. Ever since she'd been a kid, her bed was one of her favourite places. On Sundays she'd sometimes stayed in it until the afternoon, reading and drinking endless cups of tea. It was one of the things she missed most in prison. That bloody bed at the halfway house wasn't looking much better. She sighed again.

"That's a big sigh."

Startled from her thoughts, Jay looked to where Shannon stood, wearing a T-shirt that barely covered anything—and as far as Jay was concerned, the less Shannon wore the better.

Shannon smiled at the hungry look Jay knew must be in her eyes. "Something on your mind?"

"Come here and I'll show you."

"Nope. I want to know what you were sighing about, and if I come over there, we won't be doing any talking." Shannon made a point of sitting in an armchair that faced the bed, but was too far away for Jay to reach out and touch her.

Jay let out a dramatic sigh. "Fine. Have it your way."

"I always do."

"I was thinking it's a shame you're leaving so soon."

"That's sweet."

Jay grinned. "I really, really like this bed."

"Asshole!" Shannon threw a scatter cushion at her which she caught easily and laughed. "There I was, about to tell you I'd extended my trip by another day. I wish I hadn't bothered now."

"You have? Honestly?" Jay felt something warm grown inside her. She was surprised to find that it wasn't about sex or lust, just a pure happiness she hadn't felt in a long time.

She met Shannon's eyes and saw her own happiness reflected back. Happiness and something that looked a little like shyness. Overcome with the urge to hold her, Jay got off the bed and went to kneel before her. She took Shannon's hands gently in her own and lifted her face to place a soft kiss on Shannon's lips.

"What would you like to do today? I'm at your service."

"Oh, really?" Shannon pulled Jay's head forward and captured her lips in a hard kiss. As she began to deepen it, Jay pulled away.

"I love doing that, but I'd like to take you out somewhere. If you'll let me."

"Huh." Shannon regarded her with an eyebrow raised. "You don't want to fuck all day?"

"Maybe we can fuck all night instead. I'd really like to take you out somewhere. Or are you worried about being recognised?"

"No, I'm not worried. I had no idea you were this sweet. You want to take me out, huh?"

"Yes."

"Old-fashioned style?"

"What do you mean?"

"Hold open doors for me?"

"Definitely."

"Lay your cape over puddles for me to walk across?"

"You're taking the piss out of me," Jay said in mock annoyance.

"No, baby. Never." Shannon laughed, resting her arms on Jay's shoulders and kissing her mouth. "I think it's lovely. I would love to be taken out by you."

"Really?"

"Definitely." Shannon stood up and headed for the bathroom. "But when we get back, I'm going to fuck your brains out." Jay moved up quickly behind her, laughing at Shannon's squeals when her fingers found Shannon's ticklish places.

* * *

Jay stood behind Shannon with her arms wrapped tightly around her. The spray from the water didn't bother her, and it didn't seem to bother Shannon either. It had turned into a fairly warm day, now that the sun had shown its face.

Before they'd left the hotel that morning, Jay had a momentary panic. It was a long time since she'd been back in London, and suddenly she'd felt out of her depth—like a tourist in her own city. She had no idea if her old haunts were still around, and because she hadn't kept in touch with her friends from before she'd gone to prison, there was no one she could call up and ask. She had no clue where to take Shannon.

Jay sat on the huge bed. She could hear the shower running in the next room and knew Shannon would probably be out soon. Jay would still be sitting on the bed with no idea what they were going to do and looking like a great big arsehole. Shannon would probably come to her senses and quickly usher the scruffy parolee out of her hotel room and her life.

No. No, they were going out, and they were going to have a good day. Whatever came after—fleapit halfway house and life on minimum wage—this was going to be a good day. Something Jay could carry with her, a happy memory to sustain her through what was to come.

She had an idea. It was true that to all intents and purposes they were both tourists, so why didn't they have a day of doing touristy stuff? Jay didn't have a lot of cash, but that was the good thing about London. A person could do a lot for free.

There they were, on the Thames Clipper, going up to Greenwich. They had spent the morning in Shad Thames, by Tower Bridge. Shannon loved walking along the little cobbled streets as Jay tried to remember everything she had been taught in history lessons about the bridge and the former warehouses, now turned into posh flats, around them. Admittedly, she'd had to improvise on some of it and brush over other bits.

Shannon turned in her arms to brush a kiss over Jay's mouth. "Thank you for this."

"What, the dubious history lessons?"

Shannon laughed and kissed her again. Jay would have been happy for Shannon to go on kissing her forever.

"No, the day. It's been great, just walking around with you. Also, thank you for the very inventive history lesson."

"It's not over yet. Not by a long way. I've got loads more shit to make up about the Cutty Sark when we get to Greenwich." Jay smiled down at her, loving the way Shannon felt in her arms. The smell of her shampoo, clean and fresh and wonderful—just like her. *Careful, Jay. You only have this one day with her. Don't get in too deep.*

Shannon was looking at her with something in her eyes that matched the way Jay was feeling. She couldn't help herself; she bent down and placed a gentle kiss on Shannon's lips—cold and slightly wet from the spray. It had been a long time since she'd felt peace like this.

Shannon leaned into her, and they held each other all the way to Greenwich.

* * *

The hotel phone was ringing. Shannon, still wrapped in Jay's arms, untangled herself, reached for it, and knocked it to the floor. She was still tired from yesterday and last night.

"*Shit!*" She scrambled off the bed and picked up the phone. "Hello?"

"Hello, Ms Dempsey. This is your seven a.m. wake-up call."

"Thank you," she replied, heart sinking. She glanced over to the bed where Jay watched her, a look of sadness on her own face. "Hey," she said as she put the phone down.

"Hey," Jay replied softly. "You need to get ready. I'll go."

"*No!* I mean, it's fine. I have the room until two thirty. Stay, enjoy room service, sleep." She forced a joviality into her voice that she didn't feel.

"I'll stay until you leave then. I don't want to be here after you've..." *Gone. Left me. Back to your real life in Hollywood.*

"Sure," Shannon replied and nodded.

Jay watched as she went to the wardrobes and started throwing clothes into her suitcase. With a strange heaviness in her heart, she got up herself and pulled on her jeans and T-shirt.

She followed Shannon into the bathroom where they brushed their teeth together, an oddly intimate act that sent another pang of sadness through her.

Shannon gathered up her few toiletries, scooped them into a small designer bag, and zipped it up.

"You want tea?" Jay asked her.

"No, thank you," Shannon said politely, without looking up from her suitcase.

Jay felt the distance growing between them. It widened gradually, as she sat on the bed, sipping tea, watching Shannon apply makeup, force tongs through her beautiful wavy hair, watching as it steamed itself straight.

She pulled on low-slung, tight jeans, high-heeled boots, and a skimpy T-shirt. Turning, she faced Jay.

"How do I look?" she asked.

Jay grinned weakly.

"That good, huh?" she asked sarcastically and turned away again.

"No, you look great. It's just...you don't look like you."

Jay saw Shannon's body tense and realised she'd said the wrong thing. Shannon spun around.

"How the fuck would you know who I am? Jay, we spent a couple of nights screwing. Don't make it more than it is."

Jay nodded and ignored the sharp stab of pain. Shannon was right; they didn't know each other at all.

"I'm sorry. Now I'm the asshole." Shannon walked towards her, but stopped when Jay held up her hand and stepped back.

"Don't be. It's true. We don't know each other. We just fucked. A lot." She tried a smile, but it felt wooden on her face.

"We could...we could keep in touch? Maybe?" Shannon asked.

"No, I don't think so."

Shannon winced. "You're probably right."

"It's not that I don't want to, but... I mean, come on, what would we talk about?" Jay asked.

"We managed okay the last few days," Shannon replied softly.

"Shannon." Jay walked towards her. She wanted to hold her, but instead, lifted her chin with one finger and brought her face up to meet her eyes. "What would we say to each other? 'Hey, I won an Oscar!' 'Great, I stacked a bunch of shelves with baked beans.' You see?"

Shannon nodded, and the look in her eyes told Jay she did see. She nodded again and put her arms around Jay's neck. She kissed her gently on the lips. "I had a great time," she whispered.

"Yes, me too." Jay blinked once, then looked away, swallowing hard.

The phone rang again, then rang off. "That's my car," Shannon said, breaking the embrace. "Well, take care of yourself, Jay. If you're ever in Hollywood, look me up?"

Jay laughed, although it felt dangerously close to a sob. "Yes, I will. Goodbye, Shannon."

"Bye, baby." Shannon left, wheeling her suitcase behind her. Jay sat down on the bed, feeling heartbroken and unsure why. *You've only known her for five minutes. What is wrong with you?*

It was this room. She had to get out of here. She waited until she was sure Shannon would not be in the corridor, then picked up her jacket and left, pulling the door shut hard behind her.

* * *

"You look well-rested for someone who's been fucking for two straight days," Bethany said as she got in the car.

Shannon raised an eyebrow and assessed her friend. "I could say the same about you." Shannon didn't mention that her eyes looked red raw, as if she'd actually been crying for two days straight. "You okay?" she asked instead.

Bethany shrugged, blinking back more tears that threatened. "He says he'll come visit me in Kansas..."

"Hey," Shannon soothed, putting an arm around her friend and pulling her close. "I'm sure he will, Bethy." Not really knowing if it was true or not.

"I don't want to talk about it anymore. I'll just start crying again. Tell me about your girl." Bethany sat up and wiped at her eyes.

Shannon looked past her and out the window. She watched the streets of London rush by in a blur. "Not much to tell. She was great in bed and funny—it was good."

"You really liked her, huh?" Bethany asked gently as she took her friend's hand.

Shannon shrugged, her throat going tight again. "I can't understand why. I don't even know her," Shannon whispered.

Bethany pulled her into a hug and said quietly against her ear, "Sometimes, that doesn't matter. Sometimes, they just get inside you, you know?"

Shannon didn't answer. Instead, she buried her face into Bethany's shoulder and quietly began to cry.

Chapter Two

Ten Years Later

"Hey, Bethy." Shannon climbed into the passenger seat of Bethany's car and leaned across to plant a kiss on her best friend's cheek.

"Hey, honey. How are you feeling?"

"Good," Shannon replied and was pleased to discover that she meant it. "Thanks for coming to pick me up."

Bethany waved her away. "Of course I was coming to pick you up, you idiot. What, I was going to let you catch a bus?"

Bethany pulled away from the Crossroads Rehabilitation Center. Shannon watched it disappear in the rear-view mirror and felt a weight lift off her shoulders.

It had been her home for the past six months, and while the place had been a godsend, it wasn't somewhere she ever wanted to go back to. She was lucky enough that her fame had gotten her instant admission when there was usually a very long waiting list.

She felt a little guilty about that, but—like Bethany said—she was on the ropes and well on her way to being another famous person who got found dead. Crossroads had saved her life—or at least helped her save her own life.

The routine was strict and old-fashioned. Lots of exercise, lots of healthy food, and lots of therapy. She'd never been fond of routine or rules, but there Shannon had found herself strangely enjoying the comfort of it. Her therapist had made the suggestion that Shannon being in the closet created an almost unmanageable amount of stress in her life and contributed to her drug issues.

Shannon knew it hadn't helped her current situation. The stress of dodging questions and speculation about her sexuality had begun to eat at her more and more over the last few years. She wasn't sneaky by nature, and when Corin had come along, the pressure of hiding her relationship had taken its toll.

She had read all the statistics about relapse. The advice was to stay away from old hangouts, old friends, and generally anything that reminded you or tempted you back into the old life.

Shannon really didn't think it would be a problem for her, but just to be on the safe side, she planned to go away—far away—for the next few months. She never wanted to repeat that experience again. She still felt humiliated about everything that had happened. Shannon had made so many mistakes over the last year or so, and she didn't have the strength to face them all just now.

"Did you speak to your folks yet?" Bethany cut through her thoughts.

"No, I called them last week to say I was getting out. I'll call them later, when I'm settled."

"You aren't going home?" Bethany asked, surprised.

"No. I'm not ready to see them at the moment, Bethy." Shannon sighed.

She was lucky, she knew, to have parents like hers. They never judged or criticised her decisions, and sometimes she thought that was worse. They had come to see her several times in rehab, and every visit had killed her a little more. She still couldn't shake the overwhelming sense she had let them down.

She sometimes wished they would just shout at her or look disappointed or something. Instead, they supported her unconditionally and loved her just the same, and that made her feel so much worse.

"They love you, Shannon," Bethany said simply.

"I know, I know. But I need to be away. From everyone. Just for a while."

Shannon couldn't explain it. Sure, she felt a hundred times better than when she'd been admitted six months ago, but she was still fragile—broken somewhere inside. She needed to be away from everyone, as much as she loved them. She wanted to go somewhere quiet so she could lick her wounds.

Through it all her parents, brothers, Bethany, and Mark had stood by her, and she was grateful for it. More than she could ever tell them. The fact remained that she needed time alone to try and mend the broken place inside.

She wanted to put herself back together so she could come home and try to deal with the mess she had made.

"You know you can stay with me and Mark, right?" Bethany glanced at her, rubbing her knee.

Shannon placed her hand over Bethany's, feeling a massive swell of love for her best friend. "I know, Bethy. You and Mark have been so amazing, but I need to go *away*, away. Somewhere quiet and somewhere remote. It's not about you, you know."

"I know that, Shannon I just want to take care of you. You're my best friend—my sister—you know?"

"I feel the same about you, Bethy. I'm lucky to have you, I just need—"

"To go away. I know. You'll stay with us tonight?"

"Sure. As long as Mark's cooking."

Bethy elbowed her playfully, and they both laughed.

* * *

Jay waited in the short line by the checkout. Mrs Mackay and Mrs Fritz were in deep conversation, and neither noticed her standing behind them.

Jay didn't mind. In February, things were still pretty slow on the farm and she had nowhere to be. She was often restless at this time of year, though she wasn't sure why. When September came, she would be wishing for it all to be over.

Too much downtime meant too much thinking time, and she avoided that at all costs. After her two days with Shannon ten years ago, she'd bought a little radio to play in her room so she couldn't think. She still hated to be in silence.

Sometimes she came into town, to the busiest places she could find, anything to be around noise and quieten the voice inside.

"Oh, Jay!" Mrs Mackay finally saw her waiting. "I am sorry, dearie."

"No problem, Mrs Mackay. I'm not in a rush."

"How are you, Jay?" Mrs Fritz asked. "How was the pie?"

"I'm well, and the pie was delicious, Mrs Fritz," Jay said, paying for her newspaper.

"Well, you'll have to come by for dinner soon, dear."

"Honestly, Mrs Fritz, you don't have to do that."

"Nonsense." The elderly woman waved her away. "You're too thin. I know you don't eat properly."

"It's true. I was talking to George Poole the other day, and he said you hardly come by at all. When you do, it's for those horrible little ready meals," Mrs Mackay weighed in with Mrs Fritz tutting beside her.

Jay had been unsure about moving to a village as small as Topley. Immediately, the villagers had been into her business, asking her all kinds of questions. For someone with Jay's past, there were things she hadn't wanted them to find out. She'd been worried it would be difficult enough when they found out she was gay.

Mrs Mackay had been the first to ask if she had a husband. When she'd told her, unflinchingly, that no, she didn't because she was a lesbian, Mrs Mackay had barely batted an eyelid before she asked if she had a wife instead.

Some of the others in the village were less accepting—giving her a wide berth and hurrying past her in town—but eventually, once they realised that she wasn't some sex-crazed pervert, things had mellowed, and she'd been slowly absorbed into village life. No matter how nice they were in Topley though, Jay would never tell them about her time in prison. It was a constant fear someone would eventually find out.

Jay had warmed to Mrs Mackay, Mrs Fritz, and George Poole the most, and they treated her like the village bachelor. George Poole, who owned the local grocery shop, had even tried to set her up with his niece. Despite her constant excuses and, sometimes, outright refusals, he was persistent.

Jay didn't have the heart to tell him just because they were the only two lesbians in the village, it didn't mean they would automatically hit it off.

She didn't think his niece was even interested. The few times she had seen her with a girlfriend, they definitely hadn't been like Jay.

Besides, Sarah was lovely but she wasn't really Jay's type either. Not that she really knew what her type was—*Shannon*. She pushed that thought quickly from her mind. No use picking at old scabs.

When she wanted company, she drove up to London and found what she needed. A few hours of sex and always in a hotel or their place. She never took numbers and never called when they gave her theirs.

Every time, even though she told herself it was pointless, she always went to the bar where she met Shannon. Over the years it had changed hands and names a few times. She always sat in the same spot sipping her beer and waiting to hear that husky, sexy voice beside her.

She always felt the same disappointment when, after several hours, the voice never materialised, and she finally left, going out into the night to search for someone who could never touch her quite like Shannon had managed to do, all those years before.

Jay thought about Shannon a lot over the years. Sometimes, late at night when she couldn't sleep, she fired up her ancient laptop and Googled *Shannon Dempsey*. It always made her feel like a stalker, but she couldn't help herself.

One night Jay had logged on and been horrified to see details of Shannon's meltdown splashed across every news website she clicked on. Even though they'd only spent a short time together, Jay sensed Shannon was a very private person and imagined she would be humiliated by all this.

Jay had fought an overwhelming urge to get in touch with her. Thankfully, in the light of day, she had thought better of it—Shannon probably wouldn't even remember who she was, and even if she did, Jay couldn't protect her from this. She would be useless to her. She contented herself with the odd snippets about her upcoming films or photos taken in beautiful dresses. It was probably as close to Shannon as Jay would ever come again.

For the most part, she loved it there in the village. She had a good life, which was more than she'd ever dared to hope for ten years ago. Jay counted her blessings. When she'd met Shannon, she had been faced with the prospect of working for minimum wage in a dead-end job for the rest of her life.

One day she'd met Henry, and he had changed everything for her.

She'd been doing some voluntary work at one of the urban farms dotted about in London. Ponies and donkeys were the biggest animals there, and though livestock wasn't really her thing, it seemed to be the closest she would ever get to her dream.

By the time she started work at the urban farm, she was used to the funny stares and awkward silences. People avoided her, and that was fine because she wanted to be left alone.

Jay was sent to the hay barn to sweep up with Henry, a sixty-something man with a slight stoop and a beard yellowed from the roll-up cigarettes he smoked.

They struck up a friendship of sorts, though he never pried or asked for any more information than she wanted to give. Somehow, she'd found herself telling him about her former plans to be a farmer and grow hops.

'What's stopping you? You're still young.'

'Who's going to employ me? Besides, I can't afford the university fees.'

'Bollocks. If you wanted to do it, you'd do it.'

'It's not that easy.'

'Nothing in life is easy. Good things never come to those who wait, and patience isn't a virtue. How much are the fees?'

'I don't know. Why?

'Find out, then let me know.'

Jay didn't see him for a week or so after that, and the small kernel of hope that formed inside died. One day he appeared back at the farm. Everything had been a kind of fairy tale after that. Henry loaned her the money with no interest, only an agreement she would pay him back once she was set up. She went to university, then bought her farm. He worked there now with her.

She asked him once why he had helped her, and in typical Henry style, he shrugged, took down a lungful of cigarette smoke, and said simply, "Sometimes people need a hand. If you're able, you should give it to them."

It wasn't an answer, but for a few years it was the only one she got.

"Jay, dear? Still with us?"

"Sorry, Mrs Mackay, yes. What did you say?"

Mrs Mackay sighed and rummaged around beneath the counter for something. "Easter fete. Children's hospital. Tickets."

"Is it coming up already? One then, please."

Mrs Fritz frowned, slowly looking Jay up and down.

Here it comes.

"You know, Jay you're getting on a bit. Isn't it time to find a nice girl to settle down with?"

"I'm happy as I am, Mrs Fritz."

"Nonsense. You live all alone up at that farm—"

"I have Joe and Henry—"

"It's about time you found a woman," she continued as if she hadn't heard Jay. "What about Sarah, Mr Poole's niece?"

"Leave the poor girl alone. She only came in for a newspaper." Mrs Mackay found what she was looking for under the counter and handed Jay four tickets.

Jay sighed. "How much do I owe you, Mrs Mackay?"

"Four pounds, please."

Jay rummaged around in her pocket and came up with a crumpled five-pound note. She handed it over. She'd forgotten what these two got like as soon as a fete came around. She didn't expect any change from the fiver.

* * *

As soon as she walked through the door, Shannon was pulled into a bear hug by Mark.

"Hey, Shannon. It's so good to see you." He held her at arm's length to inspect her.

When they'd gotten back to the States ten years ago, Bethy had been down for weeks. One day, out of the blue, Mark had shown up at her door. He'd had an engagement ring in one hand and a suitcase in the other.

Even though Shannon was thrilled for her, she had felt a small, deep stab of pain when she thought about Jay. Shannon knew Jay would never show up at her door in the same way.

Over the years, she'd thought of Jay often. She missed her even though she'd never really had her. It became easier as time passed, and she was able to tuck her away like a secret treasure, the memory sustaining her when nothing else seemed able to.

Even now, all these years later, she remembered those dark eyes locking onto hers, holding her in their gentle depths.

"Hey, Mark. Good to see you too." She meant it. Even though he was nothing at all like Jay, Shannon was still reminded of her when she saw him. He'd proved himself to be a good friend when she needed one.

While her other so-called *friends* had slunk away after her meltdown, Mark had stood by her. He hadn't let her down.

"So," he said as she sat in the kitchen while he made tea, "Bethy said you aren't going to be staying here while you recover?"

"No, I need to be on my own for a while. Just, *alone*. You know?"

Mark nodded. "I understand what you mean. You have to heal, and you can't do that here with everyone fussing around you."

"Thanks," she said, relieved someone got it. "You don't think I'm being selfish?"

"Selfish?" Mark carried over a steaming cup of tea and placed it in front of her. "Of course not. Why would I think that? Why would anyone?"

Shannon sipped the tea and sighed contentedly. Mark made it the English way: strong with milk and sugar. Now she took hers the same way. "I don't know. I guess I've been away for six months and people—my parents—will want to see me, spend time with me."

"They'll understand." Mark blew on his tea and sipped carefully.

"I've put them through a lot."

"Shannon, look," Mark said, "you've spent your whole life being...I don't know, someone else. Someone people want you to be and it's crushed you. I think—no, I *know*—it's time for you to do something for *you*. Go away. Find out who you are, or who you want to be. Take some time. No one will think you're selfish. It's what you need."

"To find myself?" Shannon grinned from behind her mug.

"Too much?" Mark grimaced.

"No, just enough." Shannon stood up and went to him, pulling him into a hug. "I love you, Mark."

"Yeah, yeah." He pulled away, blushing. "Where will you go?"

"Sussex."

"England? Why?"

Yes, why, Shannon? Shannon didn't want to tell Mark that at some point during her stay at Crossroads her attention had turned to Jay. With that much time on your hands, your mind started to do funny things.

Shannon found herself thinking more and more about Jay. About that brief interlude so many years ago. About Jay's breath whispering over her cheek and then downwards. About the touch of Jay's fingers over her spine, gentle and strong and sure.

She found her own fingers whispering across the computer keyboard (they had an hour of computer privileges each night at seven). Before she knew it, she had managed to find Jay. Well, her farm at least. Or what she thought was Jay's farm, out in Sussex. And then, the great movie star and Oscar winner Shannon Dempsey had thought to herself, *Hey, why not just shoot down to Sussex and pay Jay a visit? If it is my Jay.* Shannon was pretty sure it was. The photo on her website had been taken from an angle and from a distance, as if she really hadn't wanted it taken at all, but Shannon was almost sure it was her.

It had taken almost thirteen hours of Internet searches, and part of her felt like the world's biggest stalker, but Shannon had done crazier things than a little googling these last few years.

Shannon thought Mark might not be totally on board with the whole Find Jay thing, so she decided to keep it to herself. She really didn't want him telling Bethy, who might tell her parents, who might stage some kind of intervention and send her back to good old Crossroads.

Instead, she shrugged and told him some of the truth. "I had a lot of spare time at Crossroads and a lot of Internet access. Sussex seemed like a nice place, and it's far enough away from here."

Mark studied her for a moment, and Shannon was sure he was going to see through her. She waited, half expecting him to guess her secret. Instead, he smiled and nodded. She was relieved he wasn't going to call her on it after all.

Hours later, after Mark made some excuse about being tired and went to bed, Shannon and Bethany were snuggled on the sofa, drinking tea.

Bethany said, "Have you spoken to Corin yet?"

At the mention of her ex-girlfriend, Shannon shuddered and scrunched her face. "No. Why would I?"

"Because you guys have a house together? Shared finances? You need to talk to her, Shannon."

"The lawyers can deal with it." She waved her hand dismissively.

"You're definitely going ahead with it all? You think you're ready to deal with that?"

"Come on, Bethy, it was over months ago. I realised when I opened a newspaper to find a featured article on my drug addiction and violent behaviour. It was a complete betrayal. I can't believe she did that to me for a few bucks. All while she was still living in the house I bought and buying crap that I paid for."

"I told you to stay clear of her," Bethany said, sipping her tea.

"I know. It seemed like a good idea at the time. She was hot and successful, and I was flattered she was interested. She used to say the most beautiful things to me."

"You bought into your own hype."

"Yes." Shannon sighed. "I guess I did. Now the jokes on me, huh?"

"No one who loves you is laughing at you, Shannon," Bethany said quietly but forcefully.

"I know." Shannon took Bethany's hand. "I don't love her anymore—but I feel so stupid. No one's going to hire me again."

"Sure they will. And you're not stupid." Bethany shook Shannon's hand. "Look at that singer. She shaved her head, went on a three-hour car chase, and she's back. She's got a new album out, for God's sake."

"You know what I'm waiting for?" Shannon met her friend's eyes.

"What?" Bethany asked softly.

"Corin's career is in the toilet right now. She's broke—she was asking me for money when I was in rehab—"

"Asshole," Bethany hissed.

"Right." Shannon laughed. "Anyway, how long do you think it'll be before she decides to out me? She'd get good money for that story."

"Shannon, right now, all you need to worry about is getting better. If she outs you, she outs you. Would it even be so bad?" Bethany rubbed her shoulder. "Aren't you sick and tired of pretending to be someone you're not?"

Shannon thought about it. It was a lie she'd lived for so long—even if was a lie by omission. Did it bother her? Would it be a relief to finally have people know?

"I don't know, Bethy," she answered honestly.

"Well," Bethany said, "whatever you do, or don't do, we love you. You know we'll be behind you, right?"

Tears welled in Shannon's eyes, and she couldn't hold them back. Bethany pulled her into her arms and stroked her hair. "It'll be okay, honey. I promise," she whispered.

* * *

Jay walked through two rows of tall hops. There wasn't a lot to see at the moment, but by March they would start to emerge and then grow steadily until September. Hopefully by then all the love and care would have paid off and she'd have a decent harvest.

She smiled to herself. Her father would be proud. This had been his dream before it was hers. One of the few times her mother had ever spoken about him, she'd told Jay he'd wanted to grow hops. Young Jay had hung on her every word. Apparently Jay's grandfather had owned a farm in Sussex but lost it through a combination of bad luck and a fondness for the drink. Jay's father had always vowed to buy it back one day. He'd died before he could.

Although this wasn't the same farm her grandfather owned, Jay thought her dad would be pleased nonetheless.

Jay had contracts with many of the local breweries, but it was several of the national ones that brought in the real money. From September to October, she would be rushed off her feet making sure the hops were picked, ready for the breweries. She usually hired a large number of seasonal workers in September, as her current staff would never cope alone.

For now she walked quietly, enjoying the crisp morning air, and watched her breath curl up like tendrils of cigarette smoke.

She'd need to go into the village today to pick up her mail. She had it delivered to the post office, as there wasn't a service this far from the village. Other than the small cottage about twenty minutes away, which mostly stayed empty, hers was the only place half an hour in any direction. While she enjoyed the solitude out there, she also enjoyed the company and easy friendship from people in the village.

If she ever did get lonely and fancy a chat, Henry had the cottage across the way. It was more of a summer house really, and Jay offered to build him a proper place, but he refused. He said he liked the summer house, and Jay believed him.

Henry was a person who never had more than he needed, and what he needed wasn't a lot.

She walked over to his place to see if he wanted anything from the village. He rarely went there, and Jay often joked he must have been a hermit in a previous life because he avoided company so much.

He was outside on the small porch, smoking a cigarette and reading.

"How's it going, Henry?"

He looked up from his book and placed one finger on it to save the page. "Can't complain. Weather's nice today. How are the hops doing?"

"Looking good. I'm going into town in a bit if you want anything?" Jay tried to see the name of the book he was reading, but most of it was covered by his hand. She thought she saw part of the title, but she had to be mistaken. Didn't she?

"Henry?"

"Yes, it's a romance novel." He was completely unashamed. And that was another thing she admired about him, his lack of interest in what others thought of him.

"Right. Thought so. Is it good?"

"It is actually. I find that romance writers, along with horror writers, are some of the most underrated of any genre. People think it can't be good fiction or good writing if it's romance or horror."

"Okay."

"You'd know that, if you bloody picked up a book once in a while." He wagged his cigarette in her direction.

"I read a book the other week," she said, feigning hurt.

Henry looked at her. He was suspicious but interested.

"*Auto Trader*," she said.

He laughed. "Get out of here. And get me some milk while you're down there."

* * *

Walking back towards the house, Jay whistled, and a large dog came bounding out of the undergrowth. She'd guessed he'd probably been on the trail of a rabbit. Joe loved to chase rabbits, which were everywhere out there. Jay had never seen him catch one, but he never gave up.

Joe was the worst hunting dog she'd ever met. She'd got him from a rescue centre several years before after he'd been dumped by the side of the motorway. He was big even as a puppy, and Jay fell in love with him on the spot.

Back at the house, she climbed into the battered old Jeep, and Joe scrabbled into the passenger seat beside her.

She drove the half hour into Topley without seeing another car and parked outside the post office. Joe stayed in the Jeep, watching her forlornly through the window.

"Hi, Sarah," she greeted the young woman behind the counter as the bell tinkled above her head.

"Hey, Jay. How are you?"

"I'm good. Just came to pick up my post. Quiet this morning," Jay replied. Usually the post office had at least one other person in it. It was the place to come for the latest gossip.

"You missed them all, I'm afraid. Mrs Fritz was in here earlier telling everyone the big news. I imagine they've all scattered to try and spread it before anyone else." Sarah grinned.

"Big news?" Jay asked as she sorted through the letters. Most of it was just the usual crap.

She came across one, her name written in a familiar scrawl, the envelope stained and crumpled. She sighed and put it in her pocket. She realised she had switched off from what Sarah was saying.

"Sorry, Sarah. What did you say?"

"I said apparently we have a big film star coming to stay in the village."

"Really?"

"Yes. Out in Bluebell Cottage, near you."

"How does Mrs Fritz know this?"

Sarah rolled her eyes. "The usual way. George Poole got a phone call from someone ordering groceries to be delivered to the cottage. At the same time, Alison Moore—you know, her that looks after the holiday cottages."

Jay nodded.

"Well, she was asked to go and open it up. Both of them were told not to tell anyone, that it's some big film star who wants to stay incognito. They don't want all the tabloids turning up."

"Wow, big news," Jay said, somewhat sarcastically. "Do we know who it is?"

"George says the name on the credit card they paid for the groceries with was Dempsey Holdings. Or something like that. I thought it might be that actress. You know, the one who lost it—Jay, are you okay?"

Sarah came around from behind the counter, looking worried, and Jay fought to get herself together. She steadied herself with one arm on the counter. "Sorry, I missed breakfast."

"Come on, sit down here." Jay allowed Sarah to put her arm around her waist and lead her to a chair near the door.

Dempsey Holdings doesn't mean it's her.

"I'll get you some water."

"No, Sarah, I'm fine." Jay held Sarah's arm gently, feeling the strength return to her legs.

"Are you sure?" Sarah was still looking at her with concern.

Just what she needed. This would be around the village in no time. "Yes, I'm sure. I'm fine. Honestly."

"Okay. Why don't you go home and get something to eat?"

"I will." Jay stood. "Sarah? Did Mrs Fritz say anything else about this film star?"

Sarah thought for a moment, then shook her head. "No, I don't think so."

"Okay, thanks. I'll see you."

"Make sure you eat something!" Sarah called after her, but Jay didn't hear. Her heart was hammering in her chest as she climbed back into the Jeep.

She sat for a moment, Joe nuzzled her shoulder and whined. It couldn't be her. Not after all this time. Why Topley of all places? Jay had followed Shannon's career loosely over the years.

She'd sometimes flicked through the gossip magazines and watched part of her acceptance speech a few years ago when she'd won an Oscar. She'd also seen her crack up live on TV. Jay had watched it only once, and not even all the way through because it was horrible. Seeing Shannon like that—so out of control—made her heart hurt.

She'd never watched one of her films though because it would have been too painful. To watch her on the screen, this woman she had touched, kissed, held. She'd known her in her most intimate moments, the sounds she made when she came, and the feel of her deep inside...

Jay took a deep breath, ran her hands through her hair, then ruffled Joe's head. "Come on. Time to go home."

Joe chuffed, as if to say he thought that that was a very good idea. The rabbits weren't going to chase themselves.

CHAPTER THREE

Shannon insisted on driving herself to the cottage. She wanted to keep a low profile, and turning up in the back of a shiny Mercedes wasn't going to help her stay off the radar for very long. Besides, she was still a country girl at heart and got embarrassed by the big shows of wealth and glamour.

She'd picked up a little hatchback car at the airport, dumped one suitcase in the back, and been on her way. She was feeling better already, as if the last year faded away the more miles she put between herself and LA. She hadn't bought more than she needed, and it was so refreshing to have a small amount of luggage and not be weighed down by so many things she didn't need.

Shannon didn't know how long she planned to stay in Sussex; she guessed that might depend on Jay.

I really think you might have lost it, Shannon. Seriously, my friend. Flying all the way over here because you can't forget about a woman you fucked ten years ago. She won't even remember you. Shannon brutally crushed the voice in her head, the one that sounded an awful lot like Corin, and Corin was someone she really didn't want to think about.

Shannon leaned forward and fiddled with the radio. She found a station that played old rock tunes—anything would do to drown out the voice. Singing along, she felt herself start to relax.

Sometime later, with the sun setting fast behind the fields, the road began to narrow, and the heavens opened.

"Great," she mumbled as she fumbled for the wipers and turned them on full.

She slowed the car and tried to concentrate on the road as darkness fell quickly. She'd forgotten how fast that happened in the country where there weren't any buildings or street lights.

As she navigated around yet another sharp bend, she misjudged the turn. The little car bumped across an uneven grass verge, and Shannon hit the brakes. She knew her reaction time was too slow and could only curse as she ploughed straight into a ditch.

"*Fuck!*" she cried and banged the steering wheel. She fumbled in her bag, looking for her cell. She turned on the interior light and saw she had no service.

"*Double fuck!*" *Now what?* She couldn't get out in this weather; she'd be soaked through in a second. She decided to wait until it stopped—if it ever stopped—and then she'd get out and walk. This was the UK. There would be a house or something somewhere close by. The place wasn't that big.

* * *

Jay turned on the narrow lane as the rain lashed against her windscreen. She squinted and thought she saw something in the distance, a dark shape with lights. Headlights. Probably a car gone into a ditch.

It wasn't an unusual sight around here. And it wouldn't be the first time Jay had had to tow somebody to the local garage. Tourists went out for a drive on roads they weren't used to, with sharp bends and narrow lanes. It got dark quickly, and with no streetlights a person could easily find themselves in a ditch. She hoped the occupants weren't hurt.

She pulled up behind the little car and left her own lights and the hazards on, so any other cars on the road could see her. Though it wasn't likely there would be any other vehicles out at this time.

Jay pulled on her heavy wax jacket and climbed down from the Jeep.

* * *

Shannon let out a scream when someone banged hard on her window. *Looks like the fucking Grim Reaper with that hood.* She shoved open the door and almost smashed it into the stranger.

"*What the fuck!*" she shouted, unmindful of the rain that pelted her. The stranger stepped back, hands out in a placating gesture.

"I saw your car in the ditch. I didn't mean to scare you."

Although muffled by the hood, something about that voice was familiar. "I drove it into the ditch. This weather sucks," Shannon said to the stranger as her heart returned to a steady beat.

"Are you hurt?" the stranger asked.

Shannon could hear kind concern in the voice and began to calm down at once. "No, I'm fine. Not so sure about the car though."

"You're getting soaked. Wait in the Jeep. I'll tow you out," the stranger said, and began walking back to her vehicle.

Shannon followed and climbed into the passenger seat, now feeling the cold. The stranger leaned in through the driver's side, started the engine, and turned the heat up to full blast. "I won't be long."

Shannon watched as the tall form got a rope from the truck and walked back to her car.

With quick efficiency, she attached the rope to both vehicles and then got back in the truck. When she pushed her hood down, Shannon's breath caught in her throat. She worked her mouth, but no sound came out. *Jay.*

Even though she'd come with the intention of seeking her out, she hadn't really been sure if she would be here, and she definitely hadn't envisaged meeting her again like this. Shannon had been sort of hoping to at least have blow-dried her hair.

Jay reversed the truck carefully. The wheels spun for a moment, gained traction, and began to pull the little hatchback out of the ditch. Without looking at Shannon, she jumped back out and went to inspect the car.

Shannon watched her, unable to quite believe that she was really there. After all the years she had thought about her, wondering how she was, thinking about finding her, and now, she was right here. Pulling Shannon's car out of a ditch. She looked the same, Shannon observed, moved the same, though she'd filled out a little since they'd last seen each other. She looked good. Where she'd been lanky before, she now looked more muscled, her face fuller. She looked damn good, in fact.

* * *

Jay recognised Shannon instantly. It was like a punch to the gut. How many years had she thought of her? Now here she was, still breathtakingly beautiful and really pissed off. Jay grinned. She looked good even when she was angry and soaked to the skin.

Jay returned to the Jeep and threw the tow rope into the backseat. Steeling herself, she turned to face Shannon and pushed down her hood.

Will she even recognise me?

"It looks okay. A couple of dents, but that seems to be it—although it's hard to tell properly in the dark. You're staying at Bluebell Cottage?"

Shannon simply nodded.

"Okay then, I'll tow you back. There's a garage in the village. I'll ask Dave to come out in the morning and take a proper look at it for you and make sure there's no serious damage."

Jay was aware Shannon hadn't spoken and was just staring at her. "What's the matter?" she asked. "Did you hit your word limit for the day?" It was out of her mouth before she thought about it.

At that, Shannon broke into a smile that almost killed Jay. Everything about those two nights and two days, almost ten years ago, came rushing back.

"Hey, Jay," Shannon finally spoke.

"Hey, Shannon." Jay's voice sounded scratchy and raw.

"Thanks for this."

"Anytime. Let me drive around the front of it so I can hook it up."

* * *

The journey to Bluebell Cottage was slow going. Jay manoeuvred the truck carefully along the narrow pitch-black lane. The wipers thumped over the windshield, sending rivers of rainwater pouring off the sides.

All the same, Shannon felt safe. Jay's presence beside her was warm and reassuring. She snuck peeks at her profile now and again. She remembered how those full, soft lips felt against hers, and on her body. *Get it together, Shannon.*

She would have to stop this right now. Chances were, Shannon was going to be seeing Jay around—*that's why I'm here*—and it wouldn't do to be swooning over her every five minutes. Besides, she might have a girlfriend—a wife even—Shannon hadn't even thought of that. The idea of it was like a knife to her gut.

"How...have you been?" Shannon asked, not knowing what else to say and trying desperately to drown out the thoughts in her mind. *Have you thought about me at all? The way I've thought about you nearly every damn day of the last ten years?* "You look really good."

"Thanks. So do you. I've been good. I've been really good. What about you? What are you doing here?"

"Didn't you see my spectacular breakdown on the Internet?" Shannon couldn't keep the bitterness out of her voice.

"I saw it. It was hard to avoid. I'm sorry that happened to you," Jay said quietly.

"It was my own fault. I fell into the trap."

"Trap?"

"I believed my own hype. I guess I got a little lost."

Jay glanced over, and Shannon couldn't meet her eyes. She didn't want to see what was in them.

"Well, it seems as though you got through it. And Shannon, I don't think you deserved it."

Shannon bit her lip, then said softly, "Looks like we're here."

Jay pulled into a short drive way, in front of a sweet-looking cottage.

"I appreciate you bringing me home."

"No problem. You go inside and get warm. I'll unhook your car."

Shannon forced herself to go inside without turning around. What she really wanted was to invite Jay inside. She didn't want her to leave just yet.

* * *

Jay watched as Shannon climbed down from the truck and walked towards the cottage. She was still so beautiful. Maybe a little too thin in the face, but she still took Jay's breath away.

Jay climbed out of the truck and went about unhooking the two vehicles. She glanced up once to see the lights go on inside the cottage.

Good, she has power. Sometimes, the electricity went out if the winds were strong, but it seemed fine tonight. Jay threw the tow rope into the back of her Jeep, climbed in, and drove away.

When she got home, Joe was waiting at the back door. He hurried over when he saw her, his tail wagging excitedly. He circled her once, then woofed. Jay opened the front door and walked into the cold house.

As she adjusted the thermostat, she thought about Shannon. Bluebell Cottage didn't have central heating. She remembered Alison complaining about how cold it was having to clean there in winter. Jay doubted Shannon had any heaters with her or wood for the burners.

Jay's first instinct was to go back over with some heaters, or at least with wood for the stove. She stopped halfway out the door. Maybe Shannon wouldn't want to see her—she hadn't looked exactly thrilled to see Jay just now—and perhaps she wanted to be left alone. Jay remembered how sad she'd seemed discussing what had happened to her in LA.

Jay sighed. She couldn't help herself. Besides, it was freezing. She couldn't leave Shannon in that house with no warmth. She should take her a couple of spare heaters. Jay would have done it for anyone. *Yeah, right.*

She sighed again and went back out to one of the sheds.

* * *

Jesus, it's freezing in here. Shannon groaned when she saw there were no radiators anywhere in the place. There was a wood stove in every room, but no wood that Shannon could see.

She was cold, and the wetness from her clothes seeped through to her skin. There had to be blankets, and there must be a shower with hot water. She hoped.

* * *

Jay knocked again on the door, seeing lights burning inside through a gap in the curtains. *What the fuck is she doing in there?* When there was still no answer, Jay began to worry. She walked around to the rear of the cottage and tried the back door. It wasn't locked, so she went inside.

"Shannon!" she called and poked her head into the small living room. Her suitcase was there, but no sign of her.

Jay climbed the stairs two at a time, reaching the top just as Shannon walked out of the bathroom. Naked. "Oh shit!" Jay quickly averted her eyes.

"*What the fuck*!" Shannon reached behind her and picked up the bath mat, trying to cover herself. "*What are you doing here*?"

"I was calling. Didn't you hear me?" Jay stared at the floor, her face hot.

"No! I was in the shower. *Jesus, Jay!*"

"Why haven't you got a towel?"

"They're in my damn suitcase, and I wasn't expecting you to come barrelling in, you moron."

Jay glanced up. The bath mat barely covered anything, and she couldn't help but be turned on. *Yes, that's lovely of you. I'm sure she's really pleased she's turning you on while she's stood soaking wet and naked in this freezing house.*

"Jay. Hey." Shannon clicked her fingers and drew Jay's eyes away from her breasts. "You're doing that thing again. The eye thing."

Jay cringed even though Shannon seemed to be smiling. "Sorry. Shit. I'll wait downstairs."

"Uh-huh. I need to go downstairs to get my suitcase."

Jay remained silent, not understanding. All she could think about was naked Shannon.

"Jay, I need to get my clothes."

"Oh! I'll bring it. You just...wait in the bedroom or something."

* * *

A short while later, Jay heard her coming down the stairs. She turned from where she was crouched over the wood burner and her breath caught in her throat at the sight of Shannon.

She had dried her hair off and tied it up loosely on her head so that parts escaped and hung in waves around her face. Although she wore a large jumper and old, threadbare leggings, Jay thought she looked more beautiful like this than in any of her pictures on the red carpet.

"Hey," Shannon said softly, coming into the room.

Jay cleared her throat. "Hi. I thought I'd get a fire going for you. Warm the place up."

Shannon came to stand beside her and held her hands close to the stove. Jay caught the clean scent of Dove soap. No expensive, upscale brands for Shannon. She smiled to herself.

"Thanks. It's so cold in here. There's no central heating."

"No, I remembered when I got home. That's why I came back. I thought you would be cold." *And I was desperate to see you again. I've spent ten years thinking about you.*

"That's sweet."

Jay shrugged and made the mistake of looking into Shannon's eyes. They were so warm and gentle, just as she remembered them. She thought she would know peace, finally, if she let herself fall into them. Shaking the thought away, she stood up.

"I brought a gas heater as well." Jay stepped back and broke the eye contact.

"Thank you. Would you like some tea?"

"I don't know. Okay, sure. Thanks." Jay stood uncertainly for a moment, before following Shannon into the kitchen.

Jay wanted to get out of there, and she wanted to stay. *Shit, I don't know what I want. This is so confusing.* She did want to stay here with Shannon, to feel that sharp, exquisite pain that came from the wanting. She would allow herself this little time with her, just a little more time.

* * *

Shannon searched the cupboards for mugs—which didn't take long as the kitchen was compact. She liked it. She liked the way everything creaked and clunked just a little bit. Her own place in LA was shiny and new, all sharp edges and crisp lines. She'd bought it because it was a good investment and because Corin loved it, but she had never really felt at home there. Not the way she was instantly comfortable and calmed by the little cottage.

"I had some groceries delivered the other day, so there should be— ah, here they are." She took down a box of tea bags and tore it open.

"Yes, it was all around the village about half an hour after you'd ordered them." Jay laughed when Shannon glanced up, one eyebrow raised.

"I was hoping to remain anonymous while I was here."

"No chance. Oh, they'll leave you alone, and it won't go outside the village. Amongst themselves they'll gossip furiously though. When they actually see you..."

"Perfect." Shannon handed Jay a mug of tea and sat at the barstool beside her. When their legs accidentally brushed, both quickly pulled away as if burned.

"What are you doing here, Shannon?" Jay asked. "I mean, why aren't you in America?"

"I had to get away. I wanted... Hell, I don't know." Shannon threw up her hands. "I didn't feel like I could breathe. I needed to clear my head." *And I wanted to see you. I missed you so much, and I don't understand it. I never understood why I couldn't get you out of my head. I can still taste you.* But she couldn't really say that, could she? Jay would think she was crazy.

"Well, it's good to see you again." Jay said. She looked uncomfortable. "I wasn't expecting to. It was—"

"A bit of a shock?"

"I definitely wasn't expecting it."

"No, me either." *That's a lie.*

"Time to go. I'll just finish the fire for you."

"I can probably figure it out if you need to go." Shannon moved away from Jay.

"It's no problem."

"I'll be fine. Really."

* * *

Jay looked into Shannon's eyes and saw they were remote. The earlier warmth in her voice was gone. Jay remembered this, remembered before when Shannon had seemed to almost tuck herself away from sight. The cool, remote film star stepping forward to take her place.

Could Jay blame her? From the little Jay had read about Shannon, she'd had a really shitty time of it. What should have been private—the addiction and breakdown—was splashed all over the newspapers, and like a wounded animal Shannon ran—ran here. And come face-to-face with her past, with Jay. Maybe she just wanted to be left alone.

No matter. Jay stood and wiped her hands on her jeans. She nodded. "Take care of yourself," she said as she left.

"You too, baby," Shannon replied softly.

* * *

Sometime later, Shannon sat on the old but very comfortable sofa, feet tucked underneath her. The logs popped in the stove and wafted the smell of smoky wood through the cottage. Feeling calm and relaxed—if she didn't think about Jay—Shannon took a sip of wine and dialled Bethany.

"Shannon! You get there okay?"

"Hey, Bethy. Yes, I'm here safe and sound. Although I drove the damn car into a ditch."

"*Oh my God!* Are you sure you're all right?" Bethany cried.

"I'm fine, really." Shannon laughed. "But guess who pulled me out of the ditch?"

"I don't know. A drop-dead gorgeous hunk?" Bethany joked.

"Is that supposed to be my fantasy or yours?" Shannon asked.

"Well, Mark is sitting right next to me, so...yours?"

Shannon laughed. "God, it's good to hear your voice, Bethy." Shannon felt tears prick the backs of her eyes. *What is wrong with me?*

"Hey, Shannon? You okay?"

"Yes, Bethany. I really am." Shannon mentally gathered herself.

"So who pulled you out of the ditch?" Bethany asked.

"Jay." For a moment, all Shannon heard was the hiss of an open line. And then: "*Jay, Jay?*"

"Uh-huh."

"*Damn.* What are the chances of that?" Bethany exclaimed softly.

Pretty good when you go hunting for her. "Tell me about it. It was so weird to see her again. It was also wonderful," Shannon said wistfully.

"Quite a coincidence. You never did get over that one, did you?" Bethany asked gently.

"I don't think so, Bethy. I mean, I'd kind of just put her to back of my mind, you know? Sometimes I'd take the memory out, when I was down, like a…a secret treasure."

"You never thought you see her again. How does she look?"

"Hot."

Both of them burst out laughing.

Bethany said, "So, what are you going to do?"

"About what?"

"About the crisis in Sudan. What do you think? About Jay, you moron!"

"Nothing." *I just wanted to see her again. I didn't really think beyond that. Did I?*

"Nothing," Bethany echoed.

"Come on, Bethy, what am I going to do? It's just like before. We don't live in the same world."

"Oh, because you're Miss Hoity-Toity Movie Star," Bethany said, sarcastically.

"No, that's not what I mean." Shannon sighed. "But it would never work. Besides, she's probably forgotten all about me. It's been ten years, and we only spent two days together."

"You didn't forget about her," Bethany pointed out.

Shannon thought back to earlier and the way Jay had looked at her when she'd been naked. And then, later, when she walked into the living room. "No, she didn't forget about me. But it's too complicated, and I just don't think I can deal with it all right now. I need to get myself straight, not even more tangled up." *Liar.*

"Well, it's your choice. But, you know, this stuff happens for a reason," Bethany persisted. "I mean, what are the chances of you bumping into her again, after all this time?"

Shannon didn't want to think about it. She already felt bad lying to Bethy. Maybe she should just tell her? *No.*

"Look, Bethy, I had a long flight. I think I'll turn in."

"Uh-huh. Run away then, Shannon," Bethany joked, but with a hint of seriousness in her voice.

"Shut up, Bethy. Goodnight."

"Night, honey."

CHAPTER FOUR

March

Jay had spent the last three weeks pretty much at the farm. She'd been to the village once, fighting the unwelcome urge to pull off into Bluebell Cottage's driveway, only allowing herself a quick glance in its direction instead.

She saw Shannon's car out front, then turned her face back to the road, scared in case Shannon materialised. She knew if she saw her, she wouldn't be strong enough to just drive on.

Since the night Shannon had turned up, Jay's mind was continually drawn to the image of her standing in the living room with her hair tied up. Without warning, and without her permission, it would flash to ten years before. Images of Shannon beneath her, astride her—her touch, her laugh. The way she had sat down next to her at the bar with that knowing look in her eyes. The one that said *"If I want you, I can have you,"* and then she did have Jay. She'd had her ever since.

Jay avoided the village just in case Shannon turned up. She knew it was childish, but there was too much pain where Shannon was concerned. Jay had grown used to the idea she would never see her again, and now she was back, she couldn't bear the idea of watching her leave again. And she would go at some point.

Shannon had a life and a career thousands of miles away. All Jay needed to do was wait it out. Wait it out and avoid the overwhelming urge to see her.

God knew she had enough to keep her busy here anyway. The weather had been bad lately. The rain hadn't let up since the night Shannon had arrived, and Jay had to watch her fledgling crops carefully to make sure they didn't perish in the harsh weather.

She would take another walk out by the stream later. It had swelled to twice its usual size, and she wanted to make sure it wasn't in danger of getting too big and flooding her land. She'd take Joe. It would be impossible to drive all the way out there with the ground so soggy. The rain seemed to have stopped for now, and the sun was peeking out, so maybe it would be a nice day. Plus, the exercise would do her good. She whistled for Joe.

"Catching flies?"

Jay turned at the sound of the voice, and smiled when she saw Henry walk slowly towards her in that way of his—like he had all the time in the world.

"Just checking on the hops."

"You've been doing a lot of that lately." Henry stopped in front of her and nodded to the plants. His laser-like gaze fell back on her. "They seem fine to me."

"You can never be too careful. With the rains and all, I need to keep a close eye on them." Jay looked away from his searching gaze and stared at the hops instead.

"Is that why you haven't been down to the village in weeks? I had to go myself the other day and suffer a grilling from Mrs Fritz and Mrs Mackay."

"Ouch. Sorry about that. How are they?"

Henry acknowledged her avoidance with a smile and replied, "They're well. They were telling me all about an actress that's staying up at Bluebell Cottage."

When Jay didn't respond, he continued, "That wouldn't be *your* actress by any chance, would it?"

Jay had told Henry about Shannon a few years ago. He was the only person she had ever told. She'd been drunk—they both had been. Henry had told her about a woman he'd met. The only woman he'd ever loved and how she'd died giving birth to his daughter.

Although she didn't have much experience with friendships, Jay understood that when someone laid themselves bare by telling you a secret that painful and terrible, you had a choice; you could either nod and commiserate, and then that was as deep as the friendship would ever go—or you could reciprocate with a secret of your own.

So she'd told him about Shannon and about what had come before. After that, they had grown closer even though they'd never talked about their secrets again.

"She's not *my* actress," Jay said more sharply than she intended. Softening slightly, she sighed. "She never was, and that's the problem. I'd rather just stay here, out of the way until she leaves."

"If you think that's the answer." Henry reached out a hand and placed it gently on her shoulder.

"It's all I've got."

"Then it'll have to do."

* * *

Shannon sat at the small breakfast bar in the kitchen, drinking tea and going through her emails.

She had about eight from Corin, ranging from sympathetic and caring to angry and threatening. Corin needed money; please, would Shannon send some? Shannon was being selfish; why wouldn't she talk to her? Finally, Shannon was a bitch, and she'd better send her some cash, or she was going to tell everyone she was a fucking dyke.

Shannon rolled her eyes, ticked the box by each email, and sent them to the trash folder where they belonged. The last thing she wanted was Corin selling her story, and Shannon knew she would. She was an asshole like that.

She'd have to deal with Corin sooner or later, but right now she just wanted a few weeks of peace. A few weeks of not having to think about her career or her bad judgement when it came to women.

Shannon scrolled down and saw several emails from her agent. They were about offers from talk shows. Apparently, everyone wanted Shannon to go on a great big soul-baring exercise on national TV. They wanted the dirt on her breakdown and subsequent spell in rehab. Her agent seemed to be on board with them. Shannon would rather stick pins in her eyes.

There was another offer of a movie that looked interesting. A low-budget affair with a young director tipped for big things. Her agent seemed to think it might be just the ticket to ease her back in. She downloaded the attached script onto her laptop. The service out here was dicey, and she didn't know when she would be able to get online again.

Shannon hadn't seen Jay since that first night, and she didn't know if she was relieved or disappointed. Jay was obviously avoiding her, and it pissed Shannon off a little. Although, she had kind of been avoiding her too. She wasn't sure why, when the whole reason for her being here was to track down Jay.

She hadn't counted on the feelings it would bring up, and Shannon wondered if she might have miscalculated the impact seeing Jay would have on her. Maybe she wasn't ready. No, that was a lie. She wanted to see Jay—even if it was just to get her out of her system. Perhaps the strength of the feelings would lessen the more time she spent with her? Be less overwhelming.

She hadn't been into the village yet, and though she told herself it was because she wanted to lay low a little longer, the truth was she was worried about seeing Jay.

She was just starting to feel better about everything. She'd gotten into a nice routine the last couple of weeks. She'd wake up around six a.m., eat breakfast, and then shower. After she'd done a little yoga, she would check her email—if the Internet didn't bug out—then take a long walk. Shannon would head back for lunch, take a nap, then read or watch movies until dinnertime.

She found an old collection of cookbooks in one of the cupboards, and she had been trying recipes from them each night. It wasn't exactly a riveting existence, but for now, it was exactly what she needed.

She glanced out the window and saw the sun had begun to peek through the clouds. She decided it might be a nice day for a walk.

The walks were her favourite part of the day, and a small part of her, a part that she barely acknowledged, always hoped she would run into Jay. Holing up in here wouldn't make that happen—Jay obviously had no intention of dropping by. Maybe Shannon could go to her? She knew from her website where the farm was, and in for one stalker penny, in for a pound, right? What if she saw her with a woman? A couple of kids...

"Don't go there, Shannon," she mumbled to herself, getting up.

She dressed in a warm sweater, jeans, and hiking boots. She pulled on her waterproof jacket and let herself out of the cottage.

The ground was soft and boggy, and Shannon was soon sweating with the effort of making her way across the fields.

After a while, she came to a stream and decided to follow it for a ways and see where it went—see if it ran in the direction of Jay's place. She could always double back if it turned out not to. She had nothing but time on her hands.

It looked like it had swelled with the rain, and the areas around it were boggy. She moved away to slightly firmer ground, enjoying her walk and the beautiful scenery.

The countryside here was breathtakingly beautiful. The fields stretched on for miles, a vibrant green, alternating with golds and browns. Even though it was nothing like Kansas, it reminded her of home. Maybe it was the space and sense of freedom she felt as she walked aimlessly. The only sounds were birds as they chatted to each other, and the only company was the occasional rabbit or fox as it darted past her or foraged close by.

At first she didn't realise she was stuck. It was only when she tried to move her leg and felt the ground hold it fast that she noticed she had walked too close to the stream. Now, she stood shin deep in thick wet mud.

Well, that's just great. Now what? She felt herself sink a few inches deeper.

* * *

As Jay got closer to the stream, she felt the ground grow softer and steered back towards the harder earth. Joe trotted on ahead, always content to go off alone. She'd never known such an independent dog.

After a few more minutes, she heard Joe bark from somewhere close by. She supposed he must have found a rabbit. Then, she heard a familiar voice.

* * *

Shannon saw the giant dog come bounding toward her. *Perfect, that's just what I need. To be mauled to death while I'm stuck in the mud.* She could see the headlines now. The dog barked and then sat down. "Hey, doggy. Nice doggy," she tried.

"His name is Joe."

Shannon spun in the direction of the voice. Forgetting she was stuck, her torso swivelled while her lower legs remained firmly in place. She wobbled for a second before falling sideways into the mud.

"*Oh shit, oh fuck!*" she managed, just before she face-planted.

Shannon wasn't sure if it was the sound of Jay's laughter that set her off, or that when she fell the dog began barking wildly; either way, she suddenly found herself upright again, with a handful of mud. And really pissed off.

"Think its funny do you, dipshit?" she snarled at Jay, then hurled the clod of mud straight at her head.

Shannon's aim was good, but not great. It hit Jay on the side of her head, then slid down her shoulder. "*Ha! Oh yes!*" She pumped the air. "Take that, motherfucker!"

* * *

Jay couldn't believe what she was seeing. Shannon Dempsey, Oscar winner and lauded actress, up to her shins in mud, swearing like a sailor and throwing clods of dirt at her. Amazing. Another one whizzed past her head, and she just about managed to dodge it.

"Shannon! Enough!" She ducked the next one. "I'm serious! Pack it in!"

"Why?" Shannon called, lobbing another lump of mud and catching Jay on the leg. "This is the best fun I've had for years!"

"Fuck's sake," Jay hissed as another missile hit her on the shoulder. "I'll leave you here. I swear I will, Shannon."

Shannon stopped with a clod in her hand, ready to go. Jay watched her weigh her options. Looking up, face streaked with mud and hair matted, Jay didn't think she'd ever seen her look so beautiful.

"You wouldn't," Shannon finally spoke.

"I would." Jay wouldn't, but Shannon didn't need to know that.

After a beat Shannon said, "Okay," and dropped the mud missile.

"Good," Jay replied and moved closer to where Shannon stood. "I'm not going to come in any further, or I'll get stuck too. Lean forward and reach out your arms."

Shannon did as she was told and felt Jay's warm hands grip hers. Jay pulled her forward, reached under her arms, and hoisted her out. For a second, Jay staggered. She tried to tell herself it was from the force and their combined weights. But that wasn't true.

Up until this moment, she'd only had the memory of how Shannon felt in her arms. Now, as she pulled Shannon tight against her, their bodies moulded together, and it was a perfect fit. Jay stumbled.

* * *

For a moment, Shannon thought they would fall. With Jay's hard, long body crushed against hers, she almost hoped they would. Instead, Shannon turned her face against Jay's neck. She smelled warm and earthy and fresh.

Jay steadied them and released her. Shannon thought she was breathing heavily and wondered if the closeness affected Jay in the same way as it did her.

"Thanks," Shannon said. "And, you know, sorry about before. With the mud."

"No problem. It was the funniest thing I've ever seen." Jay grinned.

"Get lost." Shannon laughed.

"Come on, my farm isn't too far away. You can have a shower, and I'll drive you home. I should have some clothes that'll fit you."

"Don't worry. I can walk back from here. You must be sick of coming to my rescue all the time."

"Shannon, it's no trouble. And it's only been twice. Besides, I think it's going to rain. You'll get soaked." Without looking back, Jay began walking.

Shannon followed.

* * *

The front door to Jay's house opened straight into the kitchen. On the left was a staircase and on the right was a doorway into the living room. It was bigger than the cottage Shannon was staying in, though still pretty compact.

A large kitchen table took up most of the room, with the kitchen units arranged against the wall behind it. Although it was warm inside, and the smell of wood smoke filled the air, the place was Spartan.

Spotlessly clean, free from any clutter and devoid of any personal touches that Shannon could see. It reminded her of her own home back in the States. Shannon was filled with sadness for Jay and herself. It seemed they both led lonely lives.

"Take your boots off down here. The bathroom is upstairs so you can take a shower. Come on, I'll show you."

Jay kicked off her own well-worn boots and walked up the stairs, leaving Shannon to once again follow behind.

"I'll leave you some clothes in there." Jay nodded to a closed door on the right. "Bathroom's through there. Towels are clean." Without waiting for Shannon's reply, she took off down the stairs.

* * *

Jay wasn't sure why, but she felt nervous about having Shannon in her house. It felt surreal somehow, and just so wonderful and so strange. When she heard the shower go on, she went back upstairs and found some clean clothes for her. They'd be a little too big, but fine for the journey home.

In her own bedroom Jay shed her clothes and walked into the attached bathroom. Unbidden, an image of Shannon in the shower next door came into her mind. She turned the water as cold as it would go.

* * *

Shannon came out of the bathroom feeling much better. As she reached the spare bedroom she noticed the door to the room opposite was open an inch or two. Jay stood in view with her back to Shannon, towelling her hair.

Jay was naked. Shannon's clit twitched, and her nipples hardened with memories of Jay above her, rocking against her, pushing inside her. She remembered Jay's eyes squeezed shut and the soft groans that escaped her lips—*stop it!*

Shannon quickly bolted into the bedroom and shut the door. She leaned back against it and closed her eyes. She tried to get a grip on herself. Outside the bedroom, Shannon heard Jay walk past, the floorboards creaking beneath her feet. Shannon heard her pause on the other side of the door, and she held her breath. After a moment, Jay moved away again in the direction of the stairs.

Shannon dressed quickly in the borrowed clothes which were a little too big in the waist, legs and arms. Even though they were clean they still smelled of Jay, and she closed her eyes for a moment and breathed in the scent of her. *Jesus, enough.* She felt like a lovesick teenager. She felt pathetic. Shannon towelled off her hair and followed Jay downstairs.

Jay was in the kitchen, making tea and humming along to a tune on the radio. Joe was in his bed by the door snoozing.

"Can I help?" Shannon asked from behind her.

"No, I'm fine. Did you have everything you needed?" Jay asked, bringing two mugs of tea over. "Come on. We'll drink it in there by the fire."

Shannon followed. "Thank you for the clothes. I'll make sure that I get them back to you."

"There's no rush, Shannon. Here, sit down." Jay gestured to a large comfortable-looking sofa.

The living room was much like the kitchen, no mementos or pictures of any kind. A bookcase by the fireplace held a few paperbacks but nothing else. Shannon was again struck by the emptiness of it all.

She sat down on the sofa while Jay lit a fire in the hearth. "Have you lived here long?" she asked, sipping her tea.

"About four years. I've spent most of my time concentrating on the hops. Haven't really gotten around to doing anything in here yet." Jay sounded almost apologetic.

"No, it's lovely. Really lovely."

"You're a terrible liar." Jay grinned and came to sit beside her on the sofa. "I suppose this is just a place to sleep, you know? Out there, that's where I really... I don't know. I'm waffling."

"What is that you grow?" Shannon asked. She'd noticed neat and tidy rows of something she couldn't identify as they'd walked back.

Jay leaned back against the sofa. "Hops. For beer."

"Ha! I should have guessed. Wasn't that what you were drinking in that swanky London bar when we met?"

"Yes, but only because I couldn't afford the eighty-pound champagne." Jay turned her face to Shannon. Their eyes locked as they smiled fondly at each other. In the way, Shannon thought, people did when they remember a shared moment, something just between them. The fleeting feeling of connection made her happy.

"Yes, well." Jay sat up suddenly and cleared her throat. "Pilgrims, Target, Goldings."

Shannon was lost. "You're just saying words, Jay."

"Oh, sorry. Hops. That's the types of hops I grow. And an apple orchard to supplement." Jay stood and put another log on the fire. To Shannon it didn't seem as if the fire needed it. Maybe Jay needed to do it. To get away from Shannon, break their connection.

Shannon wondered about that. The easy way they had with one another, when Jay wasn't getting spooked, that is. She remembered the ease with which they'd joked, laughed...fucked, all those years ago. But, better not to go there.

"How many acres is it?" Shannon asked as she watched Jay stare into the fire.

"One hundred. One of the biggest in the UK."

It was said with pride, and Shannon was pleased for her. "That's great. I'm proud of you. You must have worked hard."

"Thanks." Jay blushed with pride. "I never imagined I would have this, you know? When I first met you, I was...a mess, basically. I'd just got out of prison. No job, a single bedroom in a rat-hole house with six other people. And then..." Jay came and sat next to her. "It seemed to turn around."

"I'm glad for you, Jay," Shannon said softly.

"Thanks. You're doing well, aren't you? Apart from that stuff. I mean, I saw that you won that Oscar. Must have been amazing."

"Yes," Shannon said without much enthusiasm. "Did you ever end up watching any of my movies?"

"Yes, that one where you go undercover as a beauty queen..." Jay grinned.

"Still such an asshole." Shannon smiled. "I'm going to get you a box set."

"Narcissist."

"Of course. I'm an actress," Shannon said dramatically and tossed her hair.

"I hate to disappoint you, but I don't have a television."

"Get out of here! How do you not have a TV?" Looking around, she could see that Jay really didn't. "You don't even read books." She indicated the sparsely populated bookshelf. "What the hell do you do at night?"

Jay laughed. "Listen to music, go to the pub. I have a laptop."

"Have you ever even seen a movie?"

"Yes," Jay said defensively.

"Which ones?" Shannon was suspicious.

"I don't know. Lots."

"What was the last movie you saw at the theatre?"

"I don't know!"

"Think." Shannon watched her, eyes narrowed.

"...*The Waterboy*?"

"The last movie you saw at the theatre was *The Waterboy*?"

"Yes, and we call it the cinema."

"That is so tragic," Shannon said with mock sadness.

"Piss off. You're only jealous because I haven't seen any of your films."

"So you admit it! Okay, there has to be a theatre—cinema—around here."

"Nearest one is about an hour away."

"I'm taking you."

Shannon waited for Jay to decline.

"I'll take you this time. It'll give me the opportunity to show my county off."

Shannon grinned. A warm feeling started in her belly and made its way down to her toes. She felt as though she was falling back down the rabbit hole—well, jumping really. She couldn't think of anything she'd rather do more than spend time with Jay. She ignored the voice in her head telling her this wouldn't end well.

* * *

Jay stood in front of the mirror. She felt like a teenager going on a first date. Behind her on the bed lay several jumpers and shirts she had tried on and discarded.

She never cared about her appearance most of the time. Usually she would get up, pull on jeans, a T-shirt, and maybe a jumper if it was cold. This feeling was new. She wanted to look nice, wanted Shannon to think she looked nice. *This is such a bad idea.* It was too late to back out now; she was picking her up in twenty minutes. And if she was truthful with herself, backing out was the last thing on her mind.

Since yesterday, she had been trying to convince herself they were just going out as friends. That they could be friends. *Yeah, right.*

Jay took one last look in the mirror and headed downstairs.

She pulled into Shannon's driveway a short time later, parked next to the little hatchback, and climbed out.

She knocked on the door, still trying to convince herself it was normal to be this nervous when you were picking up a friend.

She gave up all pretence of this evening being a night out between friends when Shannon answered the door and her stomach flip-flopped at the sight of her.

"Hey, Jay." Shannon walked to the Jeep. She stopped and turned around when she realised Jay hadn't moved. "Are you okay?"

Jay jerked to life at the sound of her name. "Yep, let's go." She walked woodenly to the other side of the Jeep and climbed in.

Jay was lost. As soon as Shannon opened the door and Jay saw her, she knew she was well and truly fucked. Shannon wore jeans, boots, and a brown leather jacket. Her hair left loose, it waved around her shoulders, and she had the barest minimum of makeup on. Jay's heart stuttered at the sight of her, and she found it hard to catch her breath.

* * *

Shannon watched Jay's profile as she drove. She was beautiful. Shannon had the urge to reach out and stroke the back of her neck or put her hand on her thigh as she drove. She knew she was in trouble. She recalled the conversation with Bethany the night before: "You and Jay are friends now."

"Yes."

"Are you aware how deluded you sound?"

"What do you mean? We're going to the movies tomorrow night."

"Oh, Shannon," Bethany moaned. "Is she on board with this 'let's be friends' bullshit too?"

"It's not bullshit. And yes."

"Then you're both idiots." She snapped.

"Are you on your period or something?" Shannon wasn't used to the anger in her friend's voice.

"I think it's on its way, but that's not the reason I'm being mean to you. Shannon, you have never, ever gotten over this woman. You've spent the last ten years of your life thinking about her."

"That's not—"

"It *is* true. What movie are you seeing?"

Shannon was thrown off by the abrupt change in topic. "I'm not sure. I told her to pick something. You know, the last movie she saw was *The Waterboy*?"

"That's a good movie. Are you going to dinner too?"

"Yes. The deal was I pay for the movie, and she buys dinner."

"Ha! You're so in love with her."

"No, I'm not!"

"Are."

"What are we, fifteen? I told you, we're just friends," Shannon said, hotly.

"No, honey, you and I are friends. I don't remember you ever sounding this excited when we went out to see a movie."

"I don't want to talk to you anymore."

"Because you know I'm speaking the truth," Bethany said triumphantly.

"The line is breaking up. I have to go." Shannon hung up the phone.

She didn't want to think about what Bethany was saying, didn't want to admit she was right. All Shannon wanted was to spend time with Jay. She had spent years thinking about her. Thinking about her smile, her laugh, the way she moved, the way she smelled. For now, she didn't want to consider what it meant, or how she would have to leave her again.

CHAPTER FIVE

Jay pulled up parallel to the pavement and switched off the engine. "Here we are," she said and climbed out.

Shannon followed her into a small, noisy fish-and-chip shop. With faded, yellowing lino on the floor and brown moulded plastic tables and chairs, it certainly didn't look like much. A long counter lined one wall with a glass case over the top of it. Inside, Shannon could see packaged pies, bright pink sausages, and long things coated in crispy batter.

On the wall opposite was a huge mural in mosaic tiles, depicting all kinds of fish beneath the ocean. It was awful but charming at the same time.

"I know it doesn't look like much, but it does the best fish and chips in Sussex. Come on." Jay nudged her gently and walked to the counter. "What would you like?" she asked.

"I have no idea," Shannon replied. "Why don't you order for me?"

"All right. Go and find us a table."

Shannon sat near to the back. Most of the tables were full with all kinds of people. One group looked as if they were going out for the night; the two women wore sparkly dresses and the men were in suits. She'd noticed a theatre on the way so maybe they were headed there afterwards. Another couple had their heads bent close, talking urgently to one another. She watched them for a while, fiddling with the plastic tomato-shaped ketchup bottle.

"How's it going?" Jay slid into the seat opposite her and deposited a large, greasy bag of chips and a piece of fish that was covered in batter. Shannon pulled off a couple of chips that were stuck to the fish.

"Good. This place is..." She searched for the right words and came up empty.

"They taste best with salt and vinegar." Jay pushed a sticky brown bottle towards her. Gingerly, she shook it over her food, then added salt. Taking a deep breath, she picked up a chip and put it in her mouth. "Oh my God," she exclaimed, "that is amazing."

"See? Place is a shithole, but the food is great. Try some of the fish. I got you cod."

* * *

Jay brightened and felt a huge sense of relief when Shannon broke into a smile. She'd seen Shannon's face when they'd walked in, and she'd begun to panic. *Of all the places to bring a fucking film star. What were you thinking?* But, why should she care? They weren't on a date; they were just friends. *Yeah, right.*

"I had no idea there was food like this in the world." Shannon bit into some of the fish, groaning as the batter crunched between her teeth.

"I'm glad you like it," Jay said quietly, enjoying watching her eat.

"Aren't you going to eat any of yours?" Shannon looked up, her brow suddenly creased. "What? Is it all over my face?"

"What? No, no."

"Then why the look?"

"You just...looked as though you were enjoying it." Jay flushed.

"Jay, were you having dirty thoughts about me?" Shannon's eyes sparkled as she leaned forward, hands steepled where her chin rested.

"What? *No!*"

"I don't believe you." She waggled a chip in Jay's direction, then popped it in her mouth. "Eat," she commanded.

Jay grinned sheepishly, caught out, but not embarrassed. Shannon seemed quite pleased about it as well. *Careful, Jay.*

"You'll be coming here again?" She changed the subject, shaking more vinegar onto her chips.

"Maybe." Shannon picked up a chip from Jay's plate. "If you'll bring me again. I haven't been back out in the car since the ditch incident."

"Nervous?"

"A little. These roads are too narrow for me."

"Well, there isn't any public transport out here, except for a bus which goes through the village a couple of times a day. You'll be forced to drive again out of sheer boredom."

"Maybe. To be honest, I don't miss it at all. I thought I would, but I don't," Shannon said thoughtfully.

Jay wasn't sure if she was talking about driving or Hollywood. Jay felt a sudden sadness. She enjoyed being with Shannon. She hadn't realised before how lonely she was. When she was with Shannon, all of that emptiness seemed to go away.

* * *

"I think we're too late to make the film, now," Jay said.

They had talked for ages in the fish-and-chip shop with the easy way of people who had known each other for years. Shannon didn't want the evening to end so soon. For the first time in a long time, she was really enjoying herself.

They both stood by the Jeep, neither knowing quite what to say or do. Jay dug her hands into her pockets and blew out a breath. "Well, I suppose we should get back."

"Wait. Aren't we near to the ocean here?" Shannon asked.

"Yes, the beach is just up the road."

"I want to see it. Walk with me, Jay?" Shannon held out her hand, pleased when Jay took it in hers.

"You know we'll freeze down there," Jay grumbled.

"We'll be fine." Shannon snuggled into her side and put her arm around Jay's waist. Jay's arm came around her shoulders, and they walked down to the beach together.

"Look at the stars," Shannon said with wonder. Laid out above them, they twinkled and shone in the clear night sky.

"Beautiful, aren't they?" Jay responded softly.

They sat down on a bench close to the beach. Jay must have felt Shannon shiver because she took off her coat and pulled it around both of them. Shannon shuffled closer and leaned against her. Her heart beat a little faster.

"Like explosions in the sky," Shannon whispered. "Hey, what was that?" She felt Jay jerk next to her.

"Nothing."

"Are you cold?"

"No—well, yes. But it isn't that. I remember my dad saying something like that to me years ago. When I asked him where stars came from."

"Sorry. Bad memory?"

"Not at all. It's a lovely memory. I was just surprised when you said it."

"Have you spoken to your family at all?"

"My sister writes to me sometimes. She's called a few times," Jay said softly.

"That's good, right?" Shannon said brightly.

"She has problems."

Shannon followed Jay's gaze as she looked out over the ocean. She could just about make out the waves as they crashed against the shore.

"What kind of problems?" Shannon saw Jay's jaw tighten in the moonlight.

"Another story for another time. Right now I'm more interested in you. What are we doing, Shannon? Why are you here?"

Jay met her eyes, the pain laid bare, and something else. Need. White-hot need. Shannon gasped. Suddenly, her mouth was on Jay's, hungry and desperate.

Jay groaned and pushed her hands beneath Shannon's sweater, finding warm, soft flesh. Then they were at her breasts over her bra, gently gliding over her nipples.

Shannon couldn't stop herself. She reached down to Jay's fly and fumbled for her zipper. She yanked it down, slipped her hand inside, and cupped her. She felt Jay's heat in her palm; it warmed her all the way through.

"No, stop, Shannon—" Jay pulled away, moving Shannon's hand from her jeans. "We can't," she said, breathlessly.

"What? Why not?" Shannon asked, panting.

"We're on a public beach. People can see us from up there." Jay pointed.

"Okay, fine. Let's go to my place." Shannon stood, breathing heavily. Jay nodded.

* * *

What are you doing? Jay ignored her inner voice and forced her mind not to think about it. It was just sex, like before. They'd have some fun, then Shannon would go back to her life, and Jay would carry on with hers. *Liar.*

It was a terrible idea, but Jay was powerless to stop herself. She needed Shannon like she needed air. She felt like she had been suffocating. Now Shannon was here, and she could breathe again.

On the way back neither of them spoke. The air hung heavy with expectation and uncertainty.

Jay drew closer to Bluebell Cottage, signalled to turn in, and saw a large, expensive car blocking the drive. *Who is that?*

They both watched as the figure of a woman climbed out and turned to face them, shielding her eyes from Jay's headlights. She didn't turn them off.

"Oh, fuck." Shannon sighed.

"You know her?" Jay asked.

"Yes. She's my ex-girlfriend."

It was like a swift punch to the gut, though Jay refused to show it. *Ex-girlfriend?*

"I see. I'd better leave you to it." Her voice sounded hollow to her own ears.

"Jay, I'm sorry. I didn't tell her I was here. I'm not sure how she found me."

"Is she stalking you? We should call the police." Jay was overcome with a need to protect Shannon. She locked the Jeep's doors.

"No, no, it's not like that. I mean, she wasn't invited, but she isn't dangerous. Just persistent. I need to go and speak to her. Can I call you later? What's your number?"

Jay thought she saw the whole picture now, and she wasn't interested in drama. She had enough of that with her sister. "Look, Shannon, it's fine. I'll see you about, okay? This is probably for the best anyway. We shouldn't—"

"Don't say that, Jay." Shannon reached out and touched Jay's shoulder. "It's over between her and I."

"It really doesn't matter, Shannon. It's none of my business. We...we have this...*thing* between us, but it's just sexual. We could never be... We can't... I can't. Go inside now, Shannon."

Jay could see Shannon was stung by her words.

"Jay, it's not like—"

"Go, Shannon." Jay felt her defences snap back into place. She knew her face showed no emotion.

Shannon nodded once and climbed out.

* * *

What a fucking mess. Tonight she needed to deal with Corin, and tomorrow she'd find Jay and explain. *Explain what? Jay's right. You can't do this.*

She watched as Jay reversed quickly back onto the road and peeled off with a squeal of rubber.

"Oops, did I just ruin your plans?" Corin walked towards her on unsteady legs.

"Corin, you're drunk. Please tell me you didn't drive here like that."

"No, when I got here, I was sober. While I was *waiting* for you, I got drunk. Where the hell have you been all night?"

"Out." Shannon unlocked the door, and Corin followed behind.

"On a date with old MacDonald back there?" She gestured back to the door with her bottle, some of the liquid sloshing out onto her hand.

"Corin, will you be careful? Come on." She ushered her into the living room, where she half fell down into a chair.

"You didn't answer my question. Although, you don't really seem so keen on replying to me *at all* lately. What's up with that, Shan?"

"What are you doing here, Corin? Who told you where I was?"

"I'm your fucking *life partner*. I have a right to know where my sort-of wife is." Corin grinned sloppily, pleased with her stupid joke.

"Shut up, Corin. You are not even my girlfriend. I'm definitely not your sort-of wife."

"Check the deeds to the house, baby. We are entangled financially and emotionally." Corin draped her legs over the side of the chair, leaned back, and took a swig from her bottle.

She didn't look good, Shannon noted. Her face was puffy, and she'd put on weight from all the drugs and booze. Now she was bloated and pale. Corin had been beautiful. Blonde hair, blue eyes, she was America's sweetheart.

Her career had begun with a small part in a teen franchise, and with each sequel she'd made more money. Until a better teen movie had come out, and Corin found herself on the scrap heap at twenty-five.

Unlike Shannon, Corin hadn't transitioned well into adulthood. The booze and the drugs aged her beyond her years, and the roles that had always gone to her previously started going to younger, prettier women. Corin was reduced to reality TV shows and the odd bit part here and there. It had left her bitter and angry.

They'd got together at the peak of their careers, six years ago. Bethany and Mark had been wary of Corin from the start. A playgirl who liked to be photographed at all the parties, clubs, and restaurants that crawled with other famous people. She bought the tabloid magazines every week to make sure she was in them. Shannon's parents hadn't said anything, but she could see in their faces they were disappointed she'd picked this shallow person to be her partner. They were even more disappointed to see her being slowly sucked into the same life.

They'd kept their relationship quiet. Shannon had been in love and almost considered coming out publicly, but Corin had pitched a fit. She made her money from being a fantasy for young men. She'd persuaded Shannon to keep her mouth shut. Shannon couldn't believe she had ever been so weak.

She looked at Corin now, sprawled across the chair, and found it impossible to summon any anger. She just felt sorry for her. She shouldn't—Corin was an asshole—but she did all the same.

She could have easily been her: chewed up and spat back out, dazedly walking around with a hazy memory of once being a star. Confused when restaurants no longer magically ushered her to tables mere mortals had to make reservations for months in advance. Shannon was lucky. Even so, they'd both made their choices. No one had held a gun to their heads, and the old saying, 'You reap what you sow,' never seemed more apt.

Corin was nodding off. The bottle tipped dangerously toward her crotch.

"Corin, wake up, you can't stay there." She slapped her leg gently.

"What—"

"Corin, I'm serious. Get up."

Corin swung his legs back to the ground and shook her head from side to side. "Okay, okay. I am pretty drunk. Maybe I should come back in the morning." She stood and swayed.

Shannon put an arm around her waist to steady her. "You're not driving drunk. You can stay on the couch." She took the bottle from her and directed her towards the sofa. Corin flopped down, pulled off her shoes, and fell immediately to sleep.

* * *

When Jay got home, she went straight upstairs and turned the shower as cold as it would go. She stood beneath the spray until she couldn't stand it any longer, hands braced against the wall, head hanging down.

What the fuck was I thinking? What was she thinking? It was all such a mess. At the time, she'd wanted nothing more than to have sex with Shannon, lose herself in that body, in those arms again.

Thank God the ex-girlfriend had turned up and brought Jay to her senses. This kind of complication she didn't need. She had built a quiet, orderly life for herself, and now here was Shannon.

Shannon who wanted another roll in the hay, a distraction while she was here. Jay knew it would never be enough for her, not this time. Shannon would disappear back to her own life again and leave Jay here alone and empty. Living in a house that she couldn't seem to make a home no matter how much she tried.

Everything had been fine before. A little boring maybe, a little lonely, but a good life all in all.

Then, Shannon had come back. She reminded Jay of all the wanting, the needing. The great big yawning hole inside she couldn't seem to fill. *Shannon fills it.* When she was with her, it all just seemed to disappear. She felt whole again, peaceful.

Jay lay in bed for a long time before sleep came. When she woke she was tangled in the sheets. She felt exhausted. Her mouth was dry, and her head pounded. For the first time since she could remember, she didn't want to get up. She wanted to bury her head under the duvet and make it all go away.

Jay didn't have that luxury. There were too many things to do. She needed to go into the village, for one. If she went early there was less chance of running into Shannon, or God forbid, Shannon's ex.

Jay felt a hot surge of jealousy when she thought of Shannon having a girlfriend—even if they weren't together anymore. Of course Shannon had relationships. It was stupid to think that after a couple of nights with Jay she would stay celibate forever—it wasn't as if Jay had been. All the same, it still hurt her to think about it. About another woman touching her, holding her, making love to her.

The fact remained that even if the ex hadn't turned up last night, sleeping with Shannon had Bad Idea written all over it. Apart from the fact there was no future for them, Jay would be putting her at risk. If the tabloids got hold of it, they would dig into Jay's past and find out what she had done. It would put Shannon's meltdown in the shade and probably finish her career off.

Even so, when she drove past Bluebell Cottage and saw the black car from last night still in the drive, it made her heart ache. Jay tried to remind herself it was none of her business.

* * *

Shannon stood in the kitchen drinking coffee when Corin stumbled in. "You look like shit," she said, not unkindly. "Coffee?"

"Please." Corin dragged herself onto a stool and rested her head in her hands.

Shannon put the mug down in front of her and leaned back against the counter.

"Thanks," she mumbled.

"Welcome."

"Look, Shan, I'm sorry about last night."

"Just last night?"

"All of it. The emails, the texts, whatever." She gestured with her hands in a dismissive way. In a way that said she wasn't really sorry at all.

"You don't sound that sorry, Corin."

"That's because I'm a self-centred asshole." She grinned, and Shannon was reminded of Corin back when she had been twenty. Cocky and charming and just a bit dangerous.

"Threatening to out me is not cool. Two can play at that game, Corin."

"I needed cash, Shannon. Besides, all I ever used to hear from you was how you wanted to be *real*. How you didn't want to lie by omission anymore." She sipped at the coffee, not meeting Shannon's eyes.

"That's true. But, Corin, it's my decision as to when and how I come out. Not yours, and certainly not so you can make a quick buck off it. You must get some job offers."

"Oh, yes," she laughed bitterly, "reality TV mostly. Not even the good stuff. Not the dancing show. It's that one where you live in a house with a bunch of other has-beens and get filmed every hour of the day." She pushed his hands through her hair. "Hey, one of them is for a show in the UK. Maybe I could stay here? We could give it another try? What do you say? I still love you, you know."

Shannon walked around the breakfast bar and took Corin's face in her hands gently. "No, Corin. I'm sorry but no. You and I are a total car crash. You need help. You're an addict and—"

Corin jerked her head out of Shannon's hands. "Oh sure, I forgot you've been to rehab. That's like being born again, right?"

"Not at all. I've been telling you the same thing for years. I even offered to pay for it—"

"You are *not* paying for my therapy."

"Yes, outing me would be much more preferable. So you can pay for it yourself?" Shannon said bitterly.

"It probably wouldn't even matter, Shannon. Everybody loves you—even after your meltdown, all I get is people asking me about you. Never mind that my career is on the skids, it's all about *you*. It's not fucking fair."

"But blackmailing me is?" Shannon asked hotly.

When she'd met Jay, she had just got out of prison. She'd had no money, no friends, and her family wouldn't talk to her. She was never this self-pitying. Wasn't self-pitying at all. What was Shannon thinking when she'd gotten mixed up with Corin?

"I'm not blackmailing you. I just need some money to tide me over. There's this movie a friend of mine wrote. It's really good. He's trying to get backers at the moment—and he will. It's really great. He wants me for the lead. If I can just get some cash together, pay some of my debts, put some of it into this movie..."

"How much?" Against her better judgement, Shannon would give her the money. Not because she was threatening to out her, not even to get her to leave her alone. She saw the way Corin's eyes lit up when she mentioned the movie, saw the hope in them. She got a brief glimpse of who Corin had been at the beginning.

Even back then, it was still only a glimmer. Corin had always been selfish and self-centred. Shannon realised she had only ever been in love with the idea of Corin. Shannon wanted her to be something—no—someone she'd met years ago. She'd wanted her to be Jay. Corin even looked a little like Jay, and maybe Shannon held onto that and tried to mould her into something else.

Wasn't what she also had done with Jay through the years? Built her into somebody Shannon couldn't possibly know she was? A perfect woman to remember when she became so lonely and lost. Was that what she did? Instead of looking to herself for validation, she met women and tried to turn them into the perfect version of what she wanted and what she thought she needed.

There she was, halfway across the world chasing Jay. A woman she had known for a few days. She'd carved and she'd whittled and she'd made Jay into her own version of the perfect woman. She didn't know her, not really. She could be another Corin for all Shannon knew—*but she isn't,* the little voice insisted. Corin had everything and let it all turn to shit because she was so self-centred. While Jay had taken a horrible situation and somehow made herself a good, honest life. Shannon could probably learn something from her too. Corin wasn't the only one who threw everything away.

Shannon's head hurt, and all she wanted was for Corin to leave so she could be on her own again.

She doubted this movie would go anywhere. She'd heard similar stories from Corin before. A great movie a friend wrote. The friend wanted Corin to be in it. Back when Corin still had some money, she would always invest in them—one of the other reasons she was broke. Shannon would always tell her not to, but like Achilles, Corin's biggest weakness was her own vanity.

"Really? You'll let me have some cash? You're the best, Shan, really. I swear, I'll pay it all back. I'll be able to easily after we make the movie."

"I don't want it back, Corin. I want something else in return." Corin's head shot up at that, eyes narrowing. "What?"

* * *

Jay was halfway to the village when her mobile phone rang. She glanced down where it lay on the passenger seat. She didn't recognise the number. Jay let it ring off and continued driving. A few moments later, it rang again.

Cursing, she pulled over and answered it. "Hello?"

"Jay?"

"Kelly." Jay's world tilted on its axis. "What's happened?"

"I need you to come and get me."

"Where are you?"

* * *

After Corin left, Shannon poured herself another cup of coffee, then dialled Bethany.

"Hey, Shannon. Guess the line's back up."

Shannon remembered last night when she had hung up on Bethy and felt herself flush with shame. "Sorry about that, Bethy."

"Uh-huh. I forgive you. *If* you have some good gossip for me."

Shannon laughed.

"I mean it. How was your date with your buddy, Jay?"

"You were right."

"About?"

"The friendship thing."

"You slept together." It wasn't a question.

"No."

"Shannon—"

"Corin showed up before we could."

"No way! I'll bet that was awkward. What did she want?"

"Money. And it was *really* awkward."

"You didn't tell Jay about her?"

"No. Why would I? I barely know her. I realised that this morning, Bethany. I think it's the idea of her that I've always been in love with."

Bethany was silent for a moment. "Shannon, how could you love her? You spent a few nights with her. I mean, I know you had a connection, I had the same with Mark, but love?"

"That's what I mean, Bethy. I would like to be friends at least. We do have this...what did you say? Connection."

"Just be careful, honey," Bethany said, affectionately. "What happened?"

"Jay drove away. She seemed really pissed off. I gave Corin money—"

"Shannon!"

"On the condition," she continued, "that she gets out of my life. For good. No selling any stories or any other bullshit."

"What are you going to do about Jay?"

"Try and get to know her, I guess. Not like before. I want to see if there's really something there, or if I just made it up in my head. That's if she even wants to speak to me. She probably thinks I'm bad news. Maybe I am."

"Hey! That's my friend you're talking about," Bethany said.

"Anyway, what's going on with you?" Shannon was sick of talking about her fucked-up life.

They spoke for a while longer and caught up on what was happening with Bethany.

After they hung up Shannon showered, dressed, and decided to walk up to Jay's farm. She wanted to apologise for last night and explain. Even if they didn't see each other again, she didn't want Jay to think badly of her.

Jay's farm was a half-hour walk from the cottage, and luckily the weather held. When she turned into the courtyard, she didn't see Jay's Jeep. She rang the bell anyway, hoping.

When there was no answer, she started to walk around back, just as a man came from the other side. "Help you, miss?"

The guy's face was weather-beaten with deep lines carved in his forehead and cheeks.

"Hi," Shannon said, feeling awkward about being here uninvited. "I'm looking for Jay. Is she around?"

He came closer, assessing her with his faded blue eyes. "No, miss. She went to London."

"London? When?"

The man pushed his cap back on his head. "This morning. She had a family emergency. She'll be back later. Shall I tell her you came by?"

"Is she okay?" Shannon wanted to drive to London and find her. Jay didn't have any contact with her family, so it must have been serious. *God, I hope she's okay.*

"I don't know, miss. Shall I tell her you came by?"

"Sure, thanks. I'm—"

"I know who you are. I'm Henry." He stepped forward to shake her hand.

"She told you about me?"

"Yes. She told me you were in Topley."

"In a good way?"

The man smiled, then laughed, and his face was transformed. "I try not to get involved in all that. She's very private and so am I. I'll let her know you came by and that you were worried."

"Thank you, Henry."

Shannon walked back to the cottage. It must have been her sister. Jay had said she had problems, and she was the only person in her family Jay had said she still spoke to. Shannon didn't have a cell number for Jay, so she couldn't even call and check on her. Not that Jay would probably even want her to. Not after last night. Shannon couldn't blame her—the situation hadn't looked good.

Why would Jay want to go anywhere near her? Shannon had turned up fresh out of rehab with her drunk-ass ex following behind. No, anyone sane would stay away from a car crash like that. Shannon wanted to see her anyway.

CHAPTER SIX

It was late when Jay got back. She helped her sister upstairs to bed, got some ice for her own face, and sat at the kitchen table. She was beyond weary.

As soon as she'd heard Kelly's voice on the other end of the phone, she'd known her sister was in trouble. Kelly never called unless there was a problem. She preferred to write long, rambling letters when she was high on heroin—her drug of choice.

Despite that, whenever she called, Jay was powerless to stop herself from going to her.

Twice before, she'd had to pick Kelly up from the police station. Another time, she had turned up to find her sister brawling in the street with an angry landlord who was evicting her, Kelly's possessions scattered in the street around them.

This time, it was a boyfriend. He'd beaten the shit out of Kelly because he was convinced she was hiding drugs from him. Jay had walked right into the middle of it. She'd managed to pull him off her sister, taking a couple of good hits herself. She hadn't hit him back, though she was confident she could have taken him. He had the wasted body of a long-term addict and looked fifty when he was probably only half that.

Jay had to be careful. The last thing she needed was to be hauled up in court on assault charges. With her previous conviction, she would definitely do time. Instead, she'd bundled the battered Kelly into the Jeep and taken her to the hospital.

Despite practically begging her, Kelly refused to press charges or go into rehab. She agreed to come back with Jay, though the chances were she wouldn't stay long. She'd be on her way back to London to score more drugs in no time, even though she'd told Jay she wanted to get clean this time.

A knock at the door roused Jay from her dark thoughts.

* * *

Shannon saw a shadowy figure approach. She had watched from her cottage most of the evening, waiting for Jay's Jeep to go by and feeling a little like a stalker again.

A little like a stalker? Come on, Shan. That's exactly what you're turning into.

Just when she was about to go to bed, she saw Jay's truck rumble by, and relief flooded her. At least she was safe. She waited half an hour and then drove up to the farm.

The door opened, framing Jay in the doorway. Shannon gasped when she saw her face.

"Oh my God, what happened?" Without thinking, she pushed her way in, grasped Jay's face, and turned her head towards the light. Jay's jaw was red and swollen. A dark bruise was starting to form beneath the skin. Her eye was swollen and bloodshot; a dark purple bruise surrounded it.

* * *

Jay pulled her head out of Shannon's hands and stepped back. "What are you doing here?" It came out harsher than Jay meant it to. All the same, she had enough to deal with. Her sister was a mess, and here was Shannon complicating everything further.

"I..." Shannon faltered. "I came earlier to apologise for last night. I know it didn't look good. Henry told me you had a family emergency in London. I wanted to make sure you were okay."

"I am," Jay said, suddenly weary again.

"You don't look it, Jay," Shannon replied softly. "Did you go to the hospital? Those bruises look nasty."

"I did. And I'm fine. Look, Shannon, now's not a good time. Can we talk later?"

"Sure."

Jay wanted to stop her, tell her she didn't mean it, and ask her to stay. She wanted to bury herself in Shannon's arms and just let the world fade away. But she couldn't even if she wanted to. Besides, she wasn't sure if she even knew how.

For most of her life, Jay had had to rely on herself. Even though she desperately wanted to take the support Shannon offered, she was scared.

Besides, it would only make things more painful in the end. Better to endure this hurt now before they were too deeply involved than to suffer even more pain when Shannon left her again.

Jay sat back down at the table after Shannon closed the door behind her.

"Who was that?"

Jay turned to the voice on the stairs. "You're supposed to be asleep, Kelly."

"Shut up, Jay. I'm not five anymore." Kelly came to sit opposite her. "Who was it?"

"No one."

"It didn't look like no one to me. Here, put this back on your face; it's swelling up." Kelly reached across and handed her the ice pack.

"I think you need it more than me, Kelly."

Jay looked at her sister and felt the anger come up fast and hot. Whatever Jay looked like, Kelly looked ten times worse. Her face was a battered, swollen mess.

"Don't, Jay," she said softly. "I'm okay."

"He beat the shit out of you, Kelly. I should have beaten the shit out of him."

"Yes, Jay, because that would have made things better," Kelly replied harshly. "Helped the last time too, didn't it?" She pushed back angrily from the table and stomped upstairs.

"Kelly!" Jay called.

"Fuck off, Jay," she called back.

* * *

Two days passed since the night Shannon had gone to Jay. The depth of the pain had been unexpected. Shannon didn't want to think about what it meant. Not the fact Jay hadn't wanted to see her, or why she so desperately wanted to offer comfort.

It was the rage she felt when she saw what someone had done to Jay. She wanted to find them and hurt them back, which wasn't like her at all.

She didn't get those kinds of feelings about anybody. Sure, she'd thought about Jay over the years—a lot—but the more time that passed, Jay had become like a fantasy to her, a good place to go to when things hadn't been so great. She'd never expected to see her again, so when she had, she'd imprinted all of those fantasies onto the real Jay. Shannon had turned her into something she wasn't. She didn't even know her!

That night when Jay had asked her to go was for the best. From now on she would leave her alone—like Jay seemed to want.

Shannon was feeling stronger, better in body and mind. She had put back on some the weight she'd lost, and soon she would be ready to go back to her life. It was for the best.

Shannon was about to start preparing her evening meal when there was a knock at the door. "Who is it?" she called, stepping into the hall.

"It's Jay."

Shannon's heart did a quick somersault which she tried to ignore. *Doesn't mean anything. It's just biology.*

"What do you want?" she called again, not moving.

"Shannon. Please open the door?"

Something in Jay's voice had Shannon worried. She slid off the security chain and opened the door.

"What's up?" she asked as Jay stepped into the cottage. She didn't look any better than she had the other night. If anything, she looked worse. She was pale, which made the dark circles under her eyes stand out all the more. The bruises had turned an angry black and purple on her jaw and around her eye. Without thinking, Shannon reached out and stroked her face. "You look terrible."

"Thanks." Jay tried for a grin, but it didn't quite reach her eyes. "Look, I'm sorry about the other night."

"Don't worry about it." Shannon dropped her hand, turned abruptly, and walked back to the living room.

"It was rude," Jay said quietly, following her.

"Look, forget it. It's fine. Why are you here, Jay?"

As she watched Jay in the soft, muted light, Shannon's heart hurt. She was so beautiful, and for a moment the broken places inside stopped throbbing.

"I need your help. It's my sister."

"What's wrong with her?"

"She won't let me take her to the hospital—won't let me call a doctor..."

Shannon waited and watched Jay's features contort with anger, then fear, then resignation. Jay sat heavily on the sofa, head in hands. Shannon resisted the urge to go to her and instead sat in the chair across the room. "What is it?"

"She's coming off drugs. Cold turkey and I don't know what to do for her." Jay met her eyes, the torment riding close to the surface.

"Oh, Jay." Shannon did go to her then and sat close. She stroked the back of her neck, her back. "What is she on?"

"She won't tell me, but I've seen needle tracks on her arms. I know she was on heroin a few years ago, so I think it's that. *Fuck*." Jay punched the arm of the sofa. Hard. Then she leaned back with her head against the sofa and her hands over her face. "I'm sorry I came here. I don't know what I thought you would be able to do."

"I'm glad you came. I have some experience with this," she said reluctantly and waited for Jay to judge her. When Jay held her gaze, it was kind and unflinching so she continued. "Not heroin, but... Well, it doesn't matter. Point is, she needs rehab."

"I know." Jay nodded. "She won't go. She gave me a shopping list instead." Jay pulled a folded piece of paper from her jacket pocket and handed it to Shannon.

Shannon glanced down, seeing flu remedies, high-sugar energy drinks, and tablets for upset stomachs. She knew that list well. "Have you ever seen someone come off drugs?"

"No." Jay shook her head.

"It gets pretty fucked up. When did she stop?"

"She hasn't yet. What sort of sister does that make me? Letting her sit upstairs with her stash. She says she's going to stop today. That's why she needs this stuff."

"They have this in the village?"

"Yes." Jay nodded.

"Okay then. Come on." Shannon stood.

"Come on what?"

"Let's go get the stuff. We'll head back to your place and help her do this."

"You don't have to help, Shannon."

"Then why did you come to me if you didn't want my help?" Jay stayed silent and stared at the floor. Shannon softened. "Come on."

* * *

Shannon waited in the Jeep while Jay went into the small food shop. This was her first time in the village, and it looked exactly how she imagined it would.

Grey stone cottages with thatched roofs, narrow streets, and a large green space in the centre, complete with duck pond and cricket pavilion. Shit, there was even a little church with a sign out front advertising the Easter fete next month. *'Tombola! Live music! Hog roast!'*

Jay climbed back into the Jeep and handed her the plastic bag.

"Get everything?" Shannon asked.

"Yes."

"Hey?"

"*Yes?*"

"You ever go to that?" Shannon nodded in the direction of the sign.

"It's on every year. Yes, I usually go. Why?"

"I'd like to go too. Take me?"

"It isn't until next month."

"I know."

"If you want." Jay started the Jeep and drove them back to the farm. Shannon didn't know how long she would be here or even what she was doing with her life, but the idea of going to the fete with Jay made her happy.

* * *

Jay put the plastic bag on the kitchen table. "Kelly?" she called. "We're back."

Shannon looked up as a small woman descended the stairs. Her face was a mess, puffy and swollen, black and blue.

Shannon thought Kelly was probably about her own age, though she looked a decade older. The roots of her hair were dark, her natural colour most likely the same shade as Jay's. She had bleached it to within an inch of its life, so that it looked brittle and straw-like.

Her eyes were beautiful. As she came closer, Shannon saw they were the same deep chocolate as Jay's and framed by thick, long lashes.

"Hi, I'm Shannon."

Kelly took the hand offered, and Shannon noticed it was delicate and birdlike. Kelly gave her a small, shy smile, so much like Jay's.

"Yes, I know who you are. I love your films."

"Thank you. That's very kind of you to say so," Shannon replied.

"Well, this is all very surreal." Kelly turned to her older sister.

"Sorry, Kel. I was so worried, I didn't know what to do."

"I have some experience of what you're about to go through."

Shannon turned to Kelly.

"You reckon?" she responded harshly.

"Kelly," Jay warned.

"I know how trite that must sound to you. But it's true."

Kelly regarded her, her eyes glittering and hard. "Jay? Did you get my stuff?" she asked, still looking at Shannon.

"Yes, on the table."

"Thanks."

"Kelly, when was the last time you used?" Shannon asked. Kelly seemed fairly with it so it wasn't in the last few hours.

"None of your fucking business, Florence Nightingale," she shot back. "Look, I've done this before. I'll be a week with withdrawal and then fine again."

"If you've gone cold turkey before, then you obviously weren't fine again. You need rehab—"

"Give it a rest, will you? I don't need your help, and I don't want your help."

"Kelly—" Jay started to say.

Kelly spun around. "You can fuck off too, Jay. Both of you can just mind your own business." Kelly snatched the bag and went back upstairs.

"Sorry. She's embarrassed, I think," Jay said apologetically.

"Don't worry about it. Any chance of coffee?"

Kelly may have thought she was just a pampered princess who lived on another planet, but Shannon knew what was coming next. And they would need plenty of coffee for it.

Shannon sat down at the table and watched Jay move around the kitchen. There was something comforting and peaceful about it.

Shannon relaxed.

"Mama!"

Shannon and Jay both turned at the same time. Shannon watched as a small figure began a wobbling walk down the stairs.

Jay was quick. Before Shannon had even stood up, Jay was on the stairs, snatching up the little person, lifting him high in the air, and making him squeal with delight before she brought him safely back down in her arms.

She descended the stairs. The little boy had his arms wrapped around her neck.

"Shannon, meet Alfie. Alfie, meet Shannon."

What the fuck? "Hey, Alfie," Shannon said, slightly dazed.

"Mama!" he shouted in return and reached for her.

"He calls everyone that. The only word he can say at the moment. Well, that and s-h-i-t."

"How old is he?"

"Two and a half."

Shannon looked at the boy who was still reaching for her. He looked exactly like Jay, which wasn't surprising; they were clearly related. His eyes were large and brown. His hair was almost black.

"Hey, buddy." She held out her arms, and Jay passed him to her. She bounced him while he played with her necklace. "You didn't tell me about him."

Jay looked at her a little sheepishly. "Sorry. I didn't really think to tell you about Alfie. With everything else that was going on."

"It's okay. I mean, why would you? Of course you've had a life in the ten years that we've been apart—"

"No! Shannon, no." Jay's eyes widened. "He's not my son. I would never have taken you out the other night and not told you I had a kid." Jay came towards her. "He's Kelly's. Like I said, he calls everyone mama."

"Oh!" Shannon felt a huge surge of relief, unsure why. *Liar. You know exactly why.* Alfie began to wriggle in her arms, so she dropped him gently to the ground. He toddled off into the living room.

"He'll be okay in there. I babyproofed it already. Haven't gotten a stair gate yet though. Luckily Kelly already had a car seat." Jay frowned.

"Jay, you know this is a total mess, right?"

"What do you mean?"

Shannon blew out a breath. "Kelly has a baby. Going cold turkey is the worst idea. She needs a hospital, a treatment programme. Do you know the success rate of going it alone?"

Jay shook her head.

"Well...neither do I. But I know that it's pretty fuck—damn low." She glanced at the entrance to the living room and hoped Alfie hadn't heard. He didn't need another swear to add to his repertoire.

"It worked for you," Jay said quietly.

"No, Jay. It didn't."

"But you're clean."

"Now I am. Six months clean. Because I went into a programme. Not because I sweated and shook in my bedroom for a week."

"She won't go. I tried, Shannon. I told her I'd pay for it. I said I'd look after Alfie so he wouldn't have to go into care. She said no."

"I'll talk to her."

"Go ahead. She'll probably tell you the same thing."

* * *

Shannon paused outside the door to Kelly's bedroom. From inside came the sound of talking—Kelly was on the phone. Not wanting to eavesdrop, Shannon knocked. Downstairs, she heard another squeal from Alfie and Jay's laughter.

"Come in," Kelly yelled.

Shannon walked in, noticing the phone on her bedside table still lit up from her recent conversation. Kelly followed her eyes. "I wasn't trying to score if that's what you were wondering."

"It wasn't. How are you feeling?"

Kelly let the lie go. "Okay, at the moment. You met Alfie?" She picked up the magazine that was next to her on the bed and began to flick through it with feigned nonchalance.

"I did. He's a cutie."

"He looks like Jay. Weird isn't it?"

"Well, she is his aunt."

"I know, but I mean he *really, really* looks like her. It's a good thing I suppose. It'll make things easier, if...you know..."

"I don't understand," Shannon said, worrying that she did, and not sure how to handle a conversation like that.

"Never mind." Kelly sat up and turned towards Shannon. She put aside the magazine. "I imagine you're here to tell me to go to rehab."

"Yes. This really isn't the best way to do it. You need a programme, therapy—"

"What did Jay tell you? About me, I mean?" Kelly watched Shannon for her reaction. She seemed more curious than annoyed.

Shannon had the feeling another conversation was going on here, one she didn't really understand. "Not much. Nothing, in fact, before today. She told me you were going cold turkey. She told me she thought your addiction was to heroin."

"That's it?"

"That's it. She's really scared for you, Kelly."

"Jay likes to protect me." Kelly's voice held a little triumph, and something else. Something petulant. "She always has. She doesn't care what it does to her. What happens to her. She loves me."

"I can tell that," Shannon said softly.

"She'll do whatever I ask. All I have to do is click my fingers, and there she is. Like a little dog."

"Hey—"

"Do you know why she has all those bruises?"

"I imagine it has something to do with you." Shannon kept her voice even.

"My boyfriend was beating the shit out of me. He thought I was hiding drugs from him—which I was. Jay came and pulled him off. He punched her a few times." Kelly shrugged. "Want to know where Alfie was?"

Shannon didn't. She felt sick. She felt anger rise up inside. She wanted to add a few more bruises to this woman's face.

"Where?" she managed to get out.

"In the same room. Screaming his head off. He was there for most of the day. When I'm flying, I completely forget about him."

"Why are you telling me this?" Shannon kept her voice level.

Kelly shrugged again. "So you'll fuck off?"

"Kelly, I know you don't believe me, but I have been where you are."

"Oh, save it will you? I'm really not interested in your Oprah moment, Shannon. You know, I like your films, but in real life you're actually quite annoying. I don't need your help or your charity. Once I'm straight I'll be out of here so you and Jay can continue your...whatever little dyke romance you have going on." Kelly picked up the magazine again. Shannon knew when she was dismissed.

* * *

Shannon went back downstairs and into the living room. Jay was on the sofa with Alfie in her lap, reading him a story. They were both engrossed, so Shannon sat in the armchair across and watched them.

Kelly was right; they did bear a striking resemblance. She watched the baby. He was wide-eyed as Jay read the story, doing all of the characters' voices. Shannon felt unspeakably sad. *This is probably quite a few steps up from sitting in your own filth, watching your drug-addict mom get the shit beat out of her.*

Jay finished the story with a flourish. Alfie clapped his hands. "Mama!"

"I think that means he liked it." Jay looked up at her, smiling.

"I think you're right. You're pretty good at stories."

"Thanks." Jay deposited Alfie on the floor. He zeroed in on a pile of building blocks.

"She gave you a hard time?" Jay asked, studying her.

"Yes, she did."

"I'm sorry. She can be..."

"I know. Does she pull the same shit with you? Try to make you hate her?"

Jay's head snapped up. "You're a quick study."

"I'm an actress. Does she?"

"I—"

"Jay!" Kelly's voice came from upstairs.

"Shannon, would you mind—"

"Sure, I'll watch him. Go."

Jay hurried from the room, and Shannon sighed. She got up from the chair and joined Alfie on the floor, where they began building a tower with the bricks. She got to about six stories before Alfie wobbled to his feet and kicked them over.

"Again!" he cried triumphantly and laughed. Shannon couldn't help but laugh with him. She began building another tower while he watched with interest, waiting for another opportunity to kick them back down.

CHAPTER SEVEN

Jay collapsed onto the sofa next to Shannon and rested her head against the cushion.

"I left you a plate in the oven," Shannon said without looking up from her book.

For the past few days Jay hadn't slept more than a few hours. Kelly had gone hard into withdrawal, screaming for Jay at all hours. Shannon found herself dealing with Alfie. Surprisingly, she hadn't minded. He was a sweet kid.

"Thanks. And sorry."

"For what?" She looked up from her book and frowned. Jay's hair was sweaty, and the shadows were deep beneath her eyes. Shannon reached out and stroked her cheek. "You need to get some sleep, Jay," she said softly. Jay's eyes darkened—if that was possible—at her touch. She watched her swallow and flush.

"I'm okay. You should go home though. You've done so much."

"I don't mind." And she was surprised at how much she meant the words.

"But you've been looking after Alfie constantly. Cooking, washing… It's hardly what you're used to."

Shannon's eyes hardened, and her hand dropped back into her lap. "You still think I'm some spoiled princess?"

"What? No! I just meant—"

"I know what you meant, Jay."

"Obviously you don't, *Shannon*." Jay reached over and held her hand. "I meant this probably wasn't what you had in mind for your holiday."

"No, it wasn't. I wanted to help. For a long time, it's been other people helping me. Poor, broken, fucked-up little Shannon."

"You aren't fucked up." Jay still held her hand.

"Ha! Oh, you have no idea," she said bitterly. "You want to know why I'm here? Why I flew all this damn way?"

Jay nodded and held her eyes, unflinching.

"I'm running away."

"From what?" Jay whispered.

"Oh, from just about everything. I'm sure you saw all the YouTube videos of my amazing and disastrous collapse."

Jay sat up a little straighter. "I heard about it—I mean I saw a couple of things. Honestly, I couldn't watch them all. I didn't want to imagine you in that much pain and not be able to help you. I tried to ignore most of it until they moved on to someone else."

Touched, Shannon squeezed Jay's hand and sighed. "Do you want to know what happened?" She was afraid to meet Jay's eyes. To see the judgement there.

She felt Jay lift her chin gently. "Only if you want to, Shannon. What you've done—what you've been—doesn't matter to me. All I know is that you've been here for me—for Alfie and Kelly—in this moment. That tells me everything I need to know about you."

Shannon looked into her eyes. There was no judgement or censure. Only the kindness and warmth she remembered from a decade ago. Tears prickled her eyes, and she pulled away. Shannon took a deep breath. *I'll tell her. And then see if that understanding is still there.*

"Three years ago, I was shooting this movie. There was this stunt, nothing big, and I wanted to do it. I fell, landed badly, and hurt my back." Shannon watched the fire dance and remembered. "My doctor put me on these painkillers. At first, they helped, but then my back got better, and I was still taking them—lots of them."

She thought about those little pills, about holding them in her hand. How she would line them up on the table, like little soldiers—reinforcements for her addiction. She'd stare at them for a while and will herself—dare herself to throw them away. Then her mouth would fill with saliva, her skin would prickle, and she'd feel that familiar pull and that need which was almost a thirst.

Her palms would start to itch; her mouth would go dry, the flames of need licking at her belly. Before she could stop herself, she swallowed them down—one, two, three. Oh, and then the relief. Like a cool wave lapping over the flames, damping them down, reviving her. Like a woman dying of thirst, drinking down a cool glass of water. She would tell herself, *'Tomorrow. Tomorrow I'll give them up.'*

"Shannon?" Jay asked gently. She moved closer and put her arm around Shannon's shoulder.

Shannon sighed. It felt so good, this warm, strong body. "I got addicted. I was popping them like crazy. I couldn't function. I acted like a fucking idiot in public. I got snapped getting into cars without panties on, falling out of clubs—the works. I was a mess."

Jay pulled her closer still, held her gently, and kissed the top of her head.

Shannon took the comfort gratefully, leaned her head into Jay's shoulder, and sighed.

"As you can imagine, the work started drying up. No one wanted to touch me. I didn't care. I was hanging out with these rich kids—famous for sex tapes and not much else. I'd do other drugs, I'd drink... But the pills were my go-to drug. It didn't matter what else was at the party; I needed my pills. Then, one day, I woke up in a bed..." Shannon remembered it; her head had been pounding, her mind foggy. Her lips had been painfully dry and stinging. "As usual, I had no idea where I'd been, what I'd done—I was mixing the pills with booze... Anyway, I had one girl on one side of me, and another one on the other. I won't tell you who they are because they're famous too. I don't imagine they'd want me telling anyone. There was this big-screen TV on the wall and a video camera hooked up... You get the idea." Jay kissed the top of her head again. "I don't know whose idea it was, but we videoed the whole thing. I grabbed the video recorder and ran. I spent weeks terrified there was another tape out there somewhere."

"I'm so sorry, Shannon." Jay stroked her hair, held her tighter.

"No, well, it certainly wasn't a movie I wanted to make."

"Tell me the rest," Jay said quietly.

"Well, that pretty much shocked me into getting clean. I researched on the Internet about going cold turkey, and it seemed easy enough." She laughed bitterly. "Didn't want to do rehab, didn't want anyone to know I was an addict. So, I white-knuckled it. Threw up, shook, and sweated for a week—like your sister now."

"That's not the end though, is it?"

"Unfortunately not. I got clean, but it was more a case of putting a Band-Aid on a gaping wound than getting genuinely clean. Things were good for a while. I started getting jobs again. I was doing well," she said wistfully.

"I was clean, but I hadn't dealt with why I self-medicated. I was still in the closet. I was still terrified of people finding out I'm gay. The pressure was just too much, and I found myself lining those little soldiers up again. One night, I was at an awards thing. I'd taken some pills, drunk champagne before I got there. I was being interviewed on the red carpet, and I lost it. God, it was embarrassing. I was slurring, giggling, talking total shit. Then, someone behind said something snide to me, and the next thing I knew, I was throwing punches like Rocky, falling into the backdrop, swearing...*fuck*." She cringed just thinking of it. "Obviously, the whole thing went viral."

"Wow, that must have been awful."

"Icing on the cake. All of my own making. I had everything I could ever want. And I fucked it up."

"I think you're being pretty hard on yourself, Shannon. Wasn't there anyone else to help you? What about your girlfriend, Corin?"

Shannon laughed humourlessly. "Corin is a total mess herself."

The honesty and gentleness in Jay's eyes touched Shannon like nothing else ever had. Tentatively, she reached out, ran her fingers gently over Jay's forehead, along her cheek, across the edge of her mouth. Jay closed her eyes and basked in the touch like a plant only now seeing the sun.

Shannon found her mouth inches from Jay's. She mustered all her strength and pulled away quickly.

Jay's eyes flew open. Her lips were slightly parted, eyes hazy.

"Sorry," Shannon whispered.

"No," Jay said.

Shannon if wondered if she was talking about the apology or telling Shannon not to stop.

Shannon stood and went to the fireplace. She turned away from Jay. "The next thing I knew, Bethany and Mark had flown down and bundled me into rehab." Her voice sounded strange to her ears. She heard Jay get up behind her. *Don't come over here! Come over here.* When she turned, Jay stood by the window, looking out.

"Go on, Shannon. Tell me."

"Not much more to tell. I got clean, got out, and came here."

"Are you...is it working? Being here?"

"I think so," she replied softly. "I don't feel so broken. Empty. How about you?"

Jay turned and smiled crookedly at her. "Sometimes I think I'm like Humpty Dumpty... This place put me back together, but you can still see the cracks. Some of the pieces are still missing. Or maybe I never had them in the first place. I don't know."

Shannon was about to speak. Kelly's cries cut her off.

"*Jay! Jay!*"

"I'd better go and see what she wants."

"No, you need to sleep. I'll go."

* * *

Shannon walked into a wall of sweat and vomit. Kelly lay curled on the bed, jittering and clutching her stomach. She glanced over her shoulder at the sound of the door opening. She looked terrible.

"Where the fuck is Jay?" she spat.

"She needs to sleep. Sorry, you're stuck with me," Shannon replied calmly.

"Get—" Kelly gripped her stomach with both hands. She leaned over the bed and vomited into the bucket on the floor.

"Great," Shannon muttered. She crossed the room quickly and helped Kelly get back onto the bed. "What do you need?"

Kelly looked up at her, eyes glassy and her breath coming in shallow gasps.

"You to get the fuck out of my room."

"You're a real charmer, Kelly. You know that?" Shannon said dryly.

Kelly grinned, showing off a mouth full of rotten teeth. "I hate you."

"Get in line. You need one of these?" Shannon held up a box of antacids.

Kelly shook her head. "Help me get...to the bathroom."

Shannon came back around the bed and pulled Kelly up. With her arms around her waist, they made their way into the en suite. Kelly was light, almost birdlike in her arms, and Shannon had no difficulty helping her.

Back in the bedroom, Shannon lowered her gently onto the bed. Kelly was still trembling, but the jitters seemed to have calmed down a little. She looked up at Shannon with curiosity in her fevered eyes. "Why are you doing this?"

"Doing what?"

"This." She managed to wave an arm before it collapsed back onto the bed. "Helping me. I don't understand."

"You probably wouldn't."

"What's that supposed to mean? If it's to get into Jay's pants, there are probably easier ways. Besides, I saw the way she looked at you..."

"You should rest, Kelly."

"Just don't hurt her. Okay? I know she looks strong, like she can handle anything—she's had to deal with me all my life—but she's not as strong as she looks. You know?"

Shannon didn't know what to say, so she nodded instead. Kelly's eyelids began to droop then closed. Shannon backed quietly out of the room, in case she woke her.

"She thinks I hate her," Kelly said. "That I keep my distance because I think she ruined my life."

"What do you mean?" Shannon stepped forward to hear Kelly's quiet voice.

When Shannon thought she wouldn't speak again, Kelly replied, "It was the other way around."

Kelly grasped her hand, and Shannon was surprised by the strength in it. Her eyes searched Shannon's, desperate. "I've been so ashamed of what I made her do."

Shannon brushed a hand across Kelly's damp forehead. "You should sleep now."

Kelly nodded and closed her eyes. Shannon stayed for a moment longer and continued to hold her hand.

As Kelly's breathing evened out into the cadence of sleep, Shannon backed out of the room and closed the door softly behind her. She saw light shining from under the door to the spare bedroom. Jay had given Kelly her room so she could be closer to a bathroom.

Shannon knocked softly on the door. She wanted to see Jay, but she was unsure what she wanted or what she was hoping for. Jay called for her to come in.

She sat on the bed unlacing her boots. Alfie lay in the middle, fast asleep.

"Okay?" Jay asked quietly.

"Yes, she's asleep now."

Jay nodded. "You take the bed. I'll sleep on the sofa."

"There's room for both of us."

Jay didn't answer. Instead she stripped off her jeans and got under the covers. Jay lay on her back and stared up at the ceiling. Shannon stripped down to her underwear, and joined Jay and Alfie under the sheets.

She rolled onto her side, raised herself up on one arm, and watched Jay. "Hey," she whispered. Jay smiled.

"Hey," she replied.

"Jay, remember the last time we were in bed together?"

Jay's head turned sharply to face her. She didn't answer.

"Bet you didn't think the next time would be like this, huh?"

Jay grinned. "This definitely wasn't in my fantasy, no. I'm counting down the days until Alfie's new bed arrives."

Between them, Alfie stirred. They waited for him to quiet again.

"Go to sleep. I'll see you tomorrow," Shannon whispered and blew Jay a kiss without thinking. Jay automatically reached out her hand and made a fist, as if she was grabbing it up.

"Good night, Shannon."

* * *

The bell tinkled overhead as Shannon walked into the small grocery store. Jay had offered to go into the village, but she had been up half the night with Kelly, and Shannon could see she was practically dead on her feet.

Instead, she'd taken the shopping list, packed Jay off to bed, and driven her little hatchback into town with Alfie secured in the car seat in the back.

For the last few days, Kelly had seemed much better. She'd eaten a little food and even come downstairs for an hour. Shannon had been playing blocks with Alfie, and at the sight of his mother he'd shrunk away, hidden behind Shannon, and started to cry.

"He probably just needs his nap," Shannon said, hearing how pathetic it sounded.

Kelly simply smiled a small brittle smile, her eyes glittering with hardness, and replied, "No, he's just a good judge of character."

She'd stayed downstairs for a while, resting on the sofa, and watched while Shannon and Alfie played. Shannon felt sorry for her, even though she didn't really like Kelly, and even though a small, mean part of her whispered, 'You reap what you sow.'

After that, Kelly went back upstairs and didn't come down again. Shannon was relieved and felt guilty for feeling that way. Having Kelly around was like watching the approaching storm. The woman crackled with suppressed rage, bitterness, and anger. Along with the drugs, it had dug deep grooves around her eyes and mouth, and Shannon found herself holding her breath, waiting for the heavens to open with all of the vitriol bottled inside Kelly.

Even Jay seemed to sense it. Shannon noticed she watched Kelly carefully, attuned to her moods, like a keeper who loves the panther but still knows it's a wild animal and could turn on her at any time.

When Kelly wasn't around, Shannon enjoyed herself. She and Jay took turns at cooking. They went for walks on the farm with Alfie and sat in companionable silence in the evenings, reading books, and watching movies on Jay's ancient laptop.

Shannon enjoyed the walks best. Jay showed her the hops and patiently told her about each one: what it was called, when it would be harvested, what soil it liked. Jay's passion for this life reminded her of her father and how he felt about the horses.

Alfie loved being outside too. Jay bought him a little car to sit on and push along with his feet. When he eventually wore himself out from tearing around the place, one of them would end up pushing the car home with Alfie making car noises and periodically slamming his feet into the ground so that the car tipped forward. He would laugh himself silly for about five minutes.

"May I help you, miss?"

Shannon was startled from her thoughts by an older man standing close by. She realised she was staring at tinned soup moronically.

"I'm sorry. I disappeared into my own world there. I'm fine, just picking up some groceries."

"You're staying at Bluebell Cottage, aren't you?" the man asked.

Shannon shouldn't have been surprised. It was like back home in Kansas where news travelled fast.

"I'm George Poole. I've been sending up your groceries."

"Oh, thank you." Shannon wasn't really sure what to say to the man standing expectantly before her. She was saved when Alfie came barrelling over to her with a bag of candy clutched in his small hands.

"Mine!" he cried and held it up to Shannon.

This was one of a few new words and had replaced "mama" in popularity.

"He's a lovely little boy," George Poole said sincerely as he crouched down to Alfie's height and ruffled his hair. "Aren't you, little man?"

Alfie grinned and thrust out the candy. "Mine!"

"If it's all right with your mummy, you can have them."

"That's very kind, but we'll pay. And I'm a friend of the family."

"Nonsense. I don't have any grandchildren yet, so I like to indulge the little ones with a few sweets here and there." George Poole stood and regarded Shannon. He had kind eyes.

"Well, thank you then. What do you say, Alfie?"

"Fanks," the little boy replied and hurried off towards the back of the shop again.

At the register, Shannon waited while George Poole rang up her purchases and slowly packed them into shopping bags. He didn't seem to believe in hurrying.

"Will you be coming to the fete next Saturday?" he asked.

"I'd like to. I've never been before."

"You'll like ours. There's usually some music and food stalls. If you're into baking, there's a competition. First place wins a hamper from my shop. There are a few rides for the little ones."

"Well, Mr Poole, you've sold it to me. I'll definitely make sure I'm there."

"Good."

He seemed genuinely delighted. Shannon saw how someone could grow to love a place like this. It reminded her of home. With a small stab of guilt, she remembered that she hadn't yet called her parents.

The bell over the door tinkled as an elderly woman walked in.

"George—" she began.

When she spotted Shannon, the greeting died on her lips. "Oh!" she exclaimed. She moved her hand to her hair and smoothed it. "You must be the young lady staying up at Bluebell Cottage."

"Yes, I'm Shannon Dempsey. How do you do?" Shannon reached out to shake the woman's hand, which was soft and dry in hers.

"I'm Mrs Fritz. I was hoping to run into you."

"Really?" Shannon felt dread settle in her stomach. *Here we go. Nosy questions about my problems.*

"Yes. Every year at the fete we have a kissing stall. For charity. We ask all of the young people to take a turn—just for a short while, and only on the cheek. We raise money for the local children's hospital. I'm sure we'd make a packet, what with you being an actress and all."

Shannon wasn't sure what to say. It wasn't exactly what she had in mind for her quiet stay in the country. What if the newspapers got hold of it? Shannon sighed. How could she refuse a children's hospital?

As if reading her thoughts, the woman said, "Oh, I know you don't want anyone knowing you're here, dear. We wouldn't put your name on any posters or anything. Your secret's safe with us." She did a big stage wink, and Shannon was charmed.

"How could I refuse?" she replied, smiling.

"Wonderful! I'll drop over in the week to let you know what time we need you."

"Actually I'm staying with Jay at her farm."

"I know Jay," Mrs Fritz replied, a glint in her eye.

Oh great, this is going to be around the village before I've even gotten in the car.

"I'll pop up and see you there then." She turned to leave before Shannon could protest. The woman was obviously well practiced at hit-and-runs.

Shannon turned back to George Poole, who eyed her with some sympathy. "Don't worry, dearie. We gossip amongst ourselves constantly, but never with outsiders. You'll be fine." He patted her hand.

* * *

"What's going on?"

The sound of Kelly's voice started Jay, and she slid out from beneath the kitchen sink.

"Hey, Kelly." She wiped her hands on the cloth next to her and sat up. "Bit of a leaky pipe. You okay?"

"Yep." Kelly sat at the kitchen table, facing Jay. "Where's Shannon?"

"She went to the village with Alfie. They should be back soon."

"You like her," Kelly stated, leaning her chin on her hands.

"You would too, if you gave her a chance."

"That's not what I mean. I do like her. Just not the way *you* like her."

"She's a friend. That's all." Jay went back beneath the sink, hoping to end the conversation there.

"Liar. I see the way you look at her, Jay. I may be fucked in the head, but I'm not blind." When Jay didn't reply, she continued, "I think it's good. I mean, at first I was jealous. But now, I'm glad. She likes you too."

"Why were you jealous?" Jay came out from under the sink again.

Kelly shrugged, "I don't know. I've always been used to being the only woman in your life. Even though I only call when I'm in trouble. You've always been there for me whenever I needed you."

"That wouldn't change, Kelly. I'll always be there. Speaking of which, has that loser boyfriend been in touch?" Jay watched as Kelly's eyes slid away and prepared herself to be lied to.

"No. I haven't heard from him"

"Kelly."

"Fine!" she huffed. "He's called a few times—I haven't told him where I am though. Don't worry. He only wants his drugs back."

"You did steal them?" Jay scooted out from under the sink and came sit beside her sister.

"Yeah. He's shitting himself because he reckons they aren't his. Says he's holding them for someone else."

"Who?" Jay felt her skin prickle.

"A bloke in South London. He's small time anyway. Besides, he's lying. Don't worry. Who would give a load of drugs to an addict to hold on to?"

"I don't want you mixed up in something like this. These people... You don't fuck them about."

"How would you know? I can't imagine you having much to do with them."

"I was in prison with them. I know exactly what they're like. If these drugs do belong to this bloke—"

"They aren't. He's just trying to scare me into giving them back. Jay, don't worry."

"I love you, Kelly. Of course I'm worried. I'm your big sister. It's my job to look out for you." Jay nudged her gently.

"You shouldn't have to. You should have your own life. You deserve to be happy. I drag you down."

"Don't ever say that." Jay got up quickly and went to her sister, kneeling down before her. "I love you."

"I know you do." Kelly stroked her sister's face tenderly. "But you don't have to keep atoning for something that wasn't even your fault."

"It was my fault, Kelly. I should have known what was going on. I should have protected you."

"No." Kelly gently framed Jay's face with her hands and kissed her forehead.

Jay sighed and met her sister's eyes. "I feel so much guilt. Things could have been so different for you."

"It wasn't your fault. I know I've said it was in the past—I've said awful things to you. I'm clean now, and I want you to listen to me. It was not your fault. I do not blame you. I never have, Jay. I love you, too."

The simple admission stunned Jay to her core. For the longest time, she had assumed her sister hated her. That Kelly blamed her for everything that had happened, and Jay shouldered the blame readily. Knowing she was wrong shook her to her foundation. Somewhere deep inside, she felt the clouds break and a small shard of light push through. *Could it be that simple? If it is, what about Shannon?*

Jay stood and stared at a point somewhere past Kelly. She nodded. "Thank you, Kelly."

"Anytime." Kelly got up and kissed Jay on the cheek before going back upstairs.

* * *

Shannon dumped the shopping bags onto the kitchen table as Jay came through from the living room. Alfie pushed past her and scurried off into the living room. "You should have beeped. I'd have come out and given you a hand."

"Should have what?" Shannon was confused.

"Beeped—honked your horn?"

"They weren't heavy."

"How's it going?" Kelly asked.

Jay knew what she meant. "Fine. Kelly came down for half an hour then went back to bed. She seems a lot better though. Don't you think?"

"Sure," Shannon offered without much conviction. While it was true Kelly seemed to have come out the other side of withdrawal, Shannon was still not convinced that Kelly was anywhere near better. She was angry and bitter and lost. Jay wasn't stupid, and she didn't need Shannon to tell her any of this.

Shannon changed the subject and began telling her about her trip to the village as they unpacked the shopping.

"I wish I'd been there!" Jay was almost bent over with laughter.

"It isn't that funny." But Shannon was laughing too. "The woman ambushed me. I'm actually thinking of offering her a job as my agent."

"You're taking a turn in the kissing booth?" Jay started laughing again.

"I know. Not exactly a lesbian's dream job. Or a feminist's for that matter." Shannon frowned.

"It's harmless. Very tastefully done, actually," Jay replied. She tried to keep a straight face but didn't succeed.

"Knock it off will you? It's not that funny. Besides, they'll be gossiping about you like crazy right now."

"I've shacked up with the film star. I'll be a hero," Jay joked.

Shannon rolled her eyes. "You're so full of it."

"Looks like I'm missing the party." Kelly's voice came from behind. Neither had heard her come down the stairs. Shannon and Jay immediately sobered.

"Sorry, Kelly, we didn't mean to wake you."

"It's fine Jay. Nice to hear you laughing. What are we so happy about?" Kelly sat at the table, looking from one to the other.

"It's nothing really. I've somehow managed to get myself involved in the Easter fete."

"Doing what?"

"The kissing stall," Jay supplied.

Kelly was silent for a moment, then to both Shannon and Jay's surprise she burst into laughter. Shannon thought it was a beautiful sound. This time, there was no bitterness or anger in it.

"Oh Shannon, that's..." Kelly burst into another bout of laughter. Finally she managed to get control of herself and wiped the tears from her eyes.

"I'm glad the two of you find it so amusing," Shannon said, looking between both sisters.

For some reason, she had the feeling that something had happened between them. The atmosphere was lighter somehow, just like after a storm broke, the air was fresh and clear.

"Oh, by the way, Jay, I signed you up too," she said, brightly.

"What? You didn't?" Jay looked stricken.

"It's for charity. And besides, it's all very tastefully done." On the sound of fresh laughter from Kelly, Shannon made her way back outside, with Jay close on her heels.

"You didn't really did you, Shannon?" Jay put her hand on Shannon's shoulder.

"Is that a problem?" Shannon stopped and turned, smiling sweetly.

"Well, I mean..." Jay cast about.

Shannon laughed. *She's so cute.* "No, I didn't really. But it would have served you right if I had."

"Oh, thank Christ." Jay's relief was palpable. "Where are you going, anyway?"

"Back to the cottage. I have laundry to do."

"You can do it here, you know."

"About that, I think maybe I should go back to my place. Kelly seems a lot better, and I..." Shannon trailed off, surprised to discover that she didn't want to go back. She liked being with Jay. Waking up with her, eating with her. *And that's a problem.* Things were moving too fast, and Shannon wasn't sure if she was strong enough to get her heart broken if Jay didn't feel the same. It was definitely time to put some distance between them.

"Of course. You've done so much. I don't know how to thank you."

"Hey." Shannon took Jay's hands in hers. "No thanks necessary. Besides, you're taking me to the fete, right?"

"Yes, of course. If I can pry you away from the kissing stall."

Shannon laughed. "I don't think that'll be a problem. Will you be buying a kiss?" It popped out before she could stop it. Shannon blushed then hurried on. "I mean, it's for charity and all, and I—"

Without warning, Jay leaned forward and kissed her. A soft, slow, closed-mouth kiss. She pulled away too soon for Shannon's liking and said, "Looks like I'm your first customer. I don't have any cash on me though."

"You can owe me. I'll tell Mrs Fritz," Shannon whispered. She was still reeling from the kiss. Jay smiled a lazy smile that made Shannon want to be kissed again.

"I'd rather you didn't. Unless you want the whole village talking."

"You don't think they are already?"

Jay shrugged. "Maybe we can give them something to really talk about at the fete. Will you go as my date? Not friends, not acquaintances, but as my date?"

"Do you think that's a good idea?" Shannon was taken aback. She hadn't expected this from skittish Jay at all.

"Probably not. I'm sick of pretending not to feel what I do. About you, I mean. It's probably a terrible bloody idea, but..." Jay trailed off.

"Okay, then," Shannon said softly. "Let's just go with it. We'll have a holiday romance."

It was said lightly though she felt anything except light about it. She could see in Jay's eyes she felt the same. Why couldn't they make it work? She knew people in the industry who were married to people outside. Maybe a holiday romance could be the first step to something more permanent?

"I'll pick you up from your cottage?" Jay asked, hesitantly.

"Yes, okay. Saturday?"

"Saturday." Jay leaned forward and kissed her again. It was sweet and gentle—just like Jay.

CHAPTER EIGHT

"Well, well, well."

"That's it? *'Well, well, well'*?" Shannon had spent the last twenty minutes filling Bethany in on everything that had happened.

"What did you want me to say, Shannon? I *said* this was on the cards."

"That's true. What do you think? Should I have, like, a *thing* with her, or not?" She heard Bethany sigh on the other end of the line.

"Shannon, you're already having, like, a *thing* with her. You've had a thing *for* her, for ten years."

"Is that a yes?"

"It's really not my decision. I mean, can you handle saying goodbye again?"

"Maybe it doesn't need to be a goodbye this time."

"How does Jay feel about this?"

"I haven't exactly discussed it with her. She's so skittish about the whole situation. I figured we'd start slow and take it from there."

"Like, give her a bite and hope she sits down for the whole meal?"

"Does that make me crazy?"

"Ask me an easier question."

Shannon laughed. "Okay, how are you?"

"Pregnant."

"*What?*" Shannon jumped up off the sofa. "The last time we spoke you had your period!"

"I *thought* I was getting it. I was all grumpy and everything. It didn't come."

"Why didn't you call me? That is so great! Oh, Bethy, I'm so happy for you."

Bethany laughed. "We only found out two hours ago. I promise you're the first person I told."

"You're happy right? I mean, I know you weren't trying."

"I *was* happy. Mark just came home with this tiny little England soccer shirt. I don't even know where you buy something like that. I wouldn't mind, but they're terrible at it. When England is playing on TV, all I hear is Mark cursing and moaning. I don't want my child to go through the same misery."

"Maybe they'll hate sports?" Shannon offered.

This was one of the things she loved about Bethy. She could always make her laugh and take her mind off of her own problems.

"Between my parents and Mark, I don't think it'll have the option. Shannon?"

"Yes?"

"About the other thing?"

"What about it?"

"I think you should just go with it. If you really love her and she loves you, you'll find a way to make it work. Even if you can't at least you'll have tried this time. You won't be wondering about it your whole life."

Could it be that simple? She was brave enough to take the risk. Was Jay?

"Maybe. Hey, is Mark there? I want to talk to the father-to-be."

"He's here. If you can, please get him to return that shirt."

* * *

Jay was nervous. It was worse than their night at the cinema. This time, she had said the word 'date' and that put a whole new spin on it. She knew it was silly because they'd spent over a week practically living together. All the same, she was nervous.

She'd asked Kelly if she wanted to come to the fete. Kelly was improving every day, and Jay had spent the last few getting to know her sister better.

Kelly seemed content. Without the drugs and the influence of her friends, Jay was surprised to find she liked Kelly. Kelly had an almost slapstick sense of humour, and she'd had Jay in stitches with her impressions of teachers from their school years ago.

They'd talked into the night about everything, and even Alfie was warming to her. Jay hoped she would stay here on the farm. She and Kelly had missed out on so much time together, and she wanted to make it right.

Kelly turned down the fete. She wasn't quite ready to be making public appearances, and besides, weren't Jay and Shannon supposed to be on a date? Jay told her it wasn't really a date because Alfie was going with them.

Kelly was adamant about not coming, and Jay didn't want to push her. The truth was, she was looking forward to spending some time with Shannon. She was excited to be doing normal things together and getting to know her better. *And you told her it was a date.*

God, Jay was nervous.

She pulled up outside Bluebell Cottage just before noon and beeped the horn. She turned to Alfie, who sat contentedly in his car seat, and said, "Well, little man, this is it. Wish me luck."

Alfie nodded sagely and replied, "Car."

Jay looked up to see Shannon close her front door, and something gave way inside her. She couldn't describe it any better than that. The walls she had so painstakingly erected seemed to crumble at the sight of Shannon. The woman was beautiful all the way through.

"Hey," Shannon said and jumped gracefully into the Jeep. She reached back and ruffled Alfie's head.

She must have seen the expression on Jay's face because she asked, "Are you okay?"

Without answering, Jay leaned over and kissed her thoroughly. When she was finished, Shannon leaned back looking stunned. "I guess that answers my question."

"Just wanted to make sure you remembered me while you're doing all that kissing later."

"I'm pretty sure I won't be staying at the stall long, if anybody kisses me like that."

Jay laughed, and Shannon smiled.

* * *

By the time they arrived the fete was already in full swing. A stall near the entrance had a barbeque going, and the smell made Shannon's stomach rumble. She had been too nervous that morning to eat anything. The smell of barbeque reminded her she was hungry.

She looked around and thought it really was a typical English fair. The kind of thing you see on TV with a Victorian carousel off to the left which was piping out big-band music. There was a coconut shy where men stood with their girlfriends and wives next to them, launching ball after ball in an attempt to look manly by knocking the coconuts off their stands.

In the centre of the green a stage was set up, though no band was playing yet. It had rows of folding chairs lined up in front of it. Here and there, people sat eating burgers and bacon rolls and drinking beer from cans, waiting for the music to start up.

Towards the end of the green, there was a small soccer pitch with miniature goals at either end. Small children in brightly coloured shirts ran back and forth kicking a ball, while parents shouted encouragement from the side lines.

"Do you have time for something to eat before your stint on the kissing stall?" Jay leaned close to her, and Shannon could smell her fresh, clean scent.

"Definitely. I'm starving. Then I want to check out the tombola."

Jay laughed. "I've got a horrible feeling you've built this up to be far more spectacular than it actually is."

Shannon grinned. "It's pretty much all I was hoping it would be so far." Being here with Jay felt right. She couldn't remember feeling this way since she was a kid. Free, and happy, and content. She worried for her heart and that Jay wouldn't feel the same way, but Shannon was ready to give this thing between them a shot. Why not? They'd waited long enough. All she had to do was convince Jay.

"That's good." Jay leaned forward and kissed her.

"Jay, people will really be talking now." Shannon smiled.

"Let them. Burger or sausage in a bun?"

"Is that a trick question?" Shannon took Jay's hand as they walked towards the barbeque. Alfie ran ahead, stopping every few seconds to stare googly-eyed at the goings on around him.

When they got to the tombola, Shannon discovered it was basically a raffle, but she was excited all the same to win a bottle of really cheap white wine. Soon, it was time for her stint at the kissing stall. She kissed Jay goodbye and watched as she hurried after Alfie, who was making a beeline straight for the carousel.

"Hello, dear." Mrs Fritz placed a gentle hand on her elbow and guided her to the booth, lest she change her mind and run away.

"Hello, Mrs Fritz. How are you?"

"Very well dear. I'm so glad you came. Are you okay to do twenty minutes?"

"Sure, I'm looking forward to it."

"I wonder if Jay feels the same."

Shannon looked at Mrs Fritz and saw a glint in her eye. She smiled. "I think she'll be fine with it. Besides, she's busy running around after her nephew."

"Yes, someone said they'd seen a little boy in the village, and I was wondering who he might be. Is her brother—or is it sister—here as well?"

"Sister. No, she stayed up at the farm. She's been sick and didn't feel up to it."

"I'm sorry to hear that."

Shannon thought she did look sorry to hear it, despite her not-too-subtle fishing expedition.

"Maybe next time." Mrs Fritz squeezed her hand and smiled.

"Yes, maybe."

"So, you and Jay—"

"You must be Shannon Dempsey."

Another old lady came up behind them and saved Shannon from answering. Mrs Fritz looked slightly annoyed to be interrupted just as she was getting to the good stuff.

"Shannon, this is Mrs Mackay. She has the newspaper shop in the village. She's assisting me with the stall."

At the word 'assisting,' Mrs Mackay narrowed her eyes slightly. "Yes, Mrs Fritz and I run this stall *together*, every year."

"Well, I'd better go and take my place." Shannon hurried off to relieve the woman sitting on a stool as an elderly man planted a very chaste kiss on her cheek. She wasn't sure how long she could fend off the questions, but if she kept herself busy enough in the booth, maybe they wouldn't get the chance to approach her again.

* * *

Jay looked over at Shannon. She had a respectable amount of people waiting in line for her to bestow a kiss on them. Jay was half tempted to get in line herself, but she didn't think the kind of kiss she was after was suitable for a family event.

As if she knew Jay was there, Shannon caught her eye and grinned. Jay's libido fired up, and her thoughts took her back ten years to that hotel room. Jay wanted to march over to the kissing booth right now and drag Shannon off somewhere private.

Shannon adjusted her position on the stool, and the grin left her face. Her gaze burned into Jay. Was she thinking the same thing?

George Poole stepped up for his kiss, and Jay's sight line to Shannon was cut off. She sighed. It was probably for the best. Alfie tugged on her trouser leg.

"Come on, Al. Let's go and find a ride to take our mind off Miss Dempsey and her lips," she muttered.

Still gripping her trousers, Alfie made a beeline for the haunted house. There was no way she was taking him in there.

* * *

When her twenty minutes were up, Shannon quickly climbed down and prepared her excuses to make a quick exit as Mrs Fritz approached with Mrs Mackay close on her heels.

"Thank you so much for doing that, dear. You certainly had the biggest queue."

"It was my pleasure, Mrs Fritz. I'd better go and find Jay. She probably needs a break from Alfie."

"Of course, dear. I'll look out for you later on and come over for a chat." *Perfect.* Shannon hurried off and found Jay and Alfie watching the little kids playing five-a-side.

"Hey," she said and slipped her arm around Jay's waist. She kissed her.

"How was it?"

"Not too bad. I managed to avoid the old-lady inquisition."

Jay laughed. "They'll find you, Shannon. You can run but you can't hide."

"We'll see. I'm pretty good at losing the paparazzi when I have to."

"The paparazzi's got nothing on them," Jay promised.

"Alfie, are you having a good time?" Shannon bent down to talk to the little boy.

"Yes," he replied and held out his arms for Shannon to pick him up.

"We went on the carousel five times—before I bought him the candy floss." Jay reached out and ruffled his hair as he leaned his cheek against Shannon's shoulder.

"Recipe for disaster. When I was a kid, my mom and dad took me to a fair. I kept insisting on going on this roller coaster. By the third time we got to the top, and as we were coming down, I barfed everywhere."

"Fun times," Jay deadpanned.

"It really was," Shannon agreed. "What are we doing now?"

"I was going to take you on the bumper cars, but after your charming little anecdote..."

Shannon elbowed her playfully. "Come on, me and Alfie will bump the crap out of you."

"In your dreams, movie star." Jay moved away before Shannon could elbow her again.

* * *

They ended up going on the merry-go-round four times. Alfie loved the little replica fire engine—he loved all things car related. After that, they watched the Best Cake competition—Mrs Mackay was the winner—then bought some homemade ice cream and sat down to watch the band play.

The seats were all taken, so they sat to the side of the stage on a patch of grass. The sun was beginning to set on a day that had been warm and sunny. The sky over the fields beyond had turned a hazy gold. It wouldn't be long before purples and reds began to paint the sky.

Periodically, people got up to dance, and Shannon watched as they led each other around. Some of the older people did well-known ballroom steps, and it was fascinating to watch their synchronicity and style as women were spun around and then pulled back in and held close. Feet matching feet, step for step, as the dancers moved with such grace.

As an eighties soul song started up, Jay stood and held out her hands for Shannon. It was the kind of tune you couldn't help but tap your feet to, and Shannon realised she very much wanted to dance with Jay.

Jay led her out to the edge of the impromptu dance floor where they could keep an eye on Alfie who sat happily in Mrs Fritz's lap. Jay moved against her and took her hand, settling the other around her waist. Shannon moved into her, fitting her body against Jay's, reaching up and behind to clasp her free hand around Jay's neck.

She was pleased, but not surprised, to find that Jay was a good dancer. She had rhythm and an easy grace as she guided Shannon around in their small space. At some point, they changed positions so that Shannon was leading her, and soon they stopped dancing altogether. They stood still and held each other tight, swaying from side to side. Shannon was reminded of the school proms she had attended years ago. Being here with Jay, though, felt more right than it had with any of the others.

Shannon leaned her head against Jay's shoulder and breathed in the smell of her. In that moment, she didn't want to leave. She wanted to stay there forever, just rocking slowly from side to side, and feeling Jay pressed firmly against her.

The reverie was broken when Alfie sidled up to them and held up his hands for Jay to pick him up. Another song started up, this time a fast one, and Shannon watched as Jay danced Alfie around and he squealed in delight.

"You make a handsome pair," came a voice from Shannon's right. She turned to see George Poole regarding her with his kindly eyes.

"Thank you."

"You know, I had hoped to set Jay up with my niece. She's a lesbian too."

Shannon wasn't sure what to say. "Um...sorry?"

George Poole laughed. "Don't be silly. She's obviously very happy with you. I'm pleased. Jay always seems so lonely. I hope you don't think I'm speaking out of turn," he added, quickly.

"Not at all. I think you're right."

"Well, she doesn't seem very lonely now. Will you stay in the village, do you think?"

"I..." Shannon hadn't wanted to think about it. Would she stay? Could she stay? How would that even work? She was dizzy just thinking about it. If it meant being with Jay, she was willing to give it a shot.

"I'm sorry, I shouldn't pry. I'll leave that for Mrs Fritz and Mrs Mackay." He smiled and began to move away.

"Mr Poole?" Shannon asked.

"Yes, dear?"

"Thank you."

"For what?"

"I don't know. Taking care of her?"

"We always look after our own, dear." He winked and walked away.

"What was that about? Another inquisition?" Jay came up behind her, red-faced and out of breath.

"No, don't worry. It was fine. I didn't realise you were a dancing queen."

Jay grinned. "I've always enjoyed throwing a few shapes on the dance floor. You aren't a bad little mover yourself."

"Thanks. We'll have to do it again sometime. Right now, I think we'd better get back. Someone looks beat." Shannon nodded at Alfie, who had fallen fast asleep on Jay's shoulder.

"Good idea."

Back at the car, Shannon put her hand on Jay's arm. "Wait a minute. Look at that sunset."

Jay turned her head in the direction of the setting sun and smiled. "It's beautiful, isn't it?" she said softly. "We always get a lovely sunset around here."

In the hazy early evening glow, with Alfie still propped firmly against her shoulder, Jay leaned forward and kissed Shannon. It was slow and gentle, and Shannon opened her mouth to take Jay's tongue inside. When Alfie stirred, she pulled back. "We should probably wait to do that later." Her voice sounded a little breathy to her own ears.

"Yes, you're probably right. Though I don't think I'll want to stop at just a kiss." Jay smiled slowly, and Shannon's heart fluttered.

"Maybe I won't want you to," she replied.

"Right then. Let's go. Now." Jay hurriedly strapped Alfie into his car seat, and Shannon laughed as she climbed into the Jeep.

* * *

When they pulled up outside the house, Jay could see there were no lights on. She was immediately filled with a sense of foreboding. This would be just like Kelly to take off again without telling her. As if reading her thoughts, Shannon said, "Maybe she's taking a nap?"

"Maybe. Let's go inside."

The house was dark, and with the setting of the sun, a chill had begun to creep in. Jay felt around in the gloom for the light switch. She turned it on and glanced around.

The place looked like it always did—except for the dining chair. It lay on its side. Maybe Kelly had got up suddenly and it had fallen? That could have happened, sure. But why wouldn't she have righted it? Where was she? Even if she had gone for a nap, she would have put the heating on.

Jay didn't want to wake Alfie by calling out to Kelly, so she turned to Shannon. "I'm going to put him to bed. Can you check her room?

"Sure." Shannon didn't ask any questions. They were both thinking the same thing. Kelly had taken the opportunity while they were at the fete to do a flit.

* * *

Although Jay was optimistic about Kelly's recovery, Shannon knew better. She knew about being an addict, about that persistent itch in the back of your brain, the way you got consumed with the thought of it, like an old record needle stuck in the groove, scratching over it again and again until it drove you crazy. And then, the need would overwhelm you, until you could do nothing but seek out a fix.

As Shannon suspected, Kelly wasn't in her room. She met Jay on the landing and shook her head. Jay closed her eyes for a moment, and she briefly sagged against the wall. Shannon wanted nothing more in that moment than to go to her. Instead, she said, "All of her clothes are still there, so I guess she's coming back."

"What?" Jay's eyes flew open. "This doesn't make sense."

"What do you mean?"

"Shannon, you've been staying here for long enough. How many buses have you seen?"

"She might have taken a taxi—Jay! Where are you going?"

Instead of answering, Jay jogged down the stairs and picked up the phone. "I'm dialling the last number—hello? Oh, sorry, Henry. I didn't mean to call you... No... No, we went to the fete. What time? No, that's all right, Henry. Thanks." Jay put the receiver down gently and turned to Shannon. For the first time Shannon had known her, Jay looked afraid.

Shannon went to Jay and took her hands. They were ice cold. "You're scaring me. What happened?"

"Henry saw a car drive off earlier—about an hour after we went to the fete. He was in the lower fields, checking on the crops."

"Someone picked her up? That explains it then. I'm so sorry."

"No, you don't understand. Henry said it was a nice car—an expensive car. No one Kelly knows can afford a bike, let alone a *BMW*. I know what you think, but I don't think she left to score drugs. When she's done it before, she usually nicks anything worth selling from here—"

"That's why you don't have much?"

"I got tired of replacing it all the time."

"Oh, Jay."

"It's okay, Shannon. She told me that her boyfriend—the one she wanted me to get her from—he said the drugs she took weren't his."

"Whose were they?"

"They belonged to a man from South London. Small time she said. She said she thought her boyfriend was lying, and I believed her."

"Shit. Do you think he came for her? How much did she take?"

"I don't know!" Jay cried. "I never even bothered to fucking ask! Once again. Kelly feeds me shit, and I swallow it all down—"

"This isn't your fault!"

"Then whose is it?" Jay was shouting now.

Shannon couldn't bear to see the pain in her eyes anymore and went to her.

"We'll find her." She was surprised at how easily Jay came into her arms.

"I have to find her, Shannon. Before—"

"It's okay. We will, I promise." Shannon rubbed her back, feeling how close to breaking she was and knowing that she was helpless to do more than hold her.

* * *

"Your tea's gone cold. Would you like another?" Shannon sat at the kitchen table across from Jay. It had been about an hour since the police arrived and took their statements. Jay gave them as much information as she could—which wasn't a lot. She had the address of where she collected Kelly from, but little else. She didn't even know her boyfriend's name.

Henry was interviewed as well and was able to give them a description of the car, but unable to provide any details about the number plate or the occupants.

All they could do now was wait.

"No, thanks," Jay said. She was terrified—torturing herself with thoughts of what might be happening to Kelly.

Jay had only ever felt this helpless once before in her life. That time, it was to do with Kelly as well. What if they didn't get her back? What if they weren't even looking for her? She was just a drug addict to the police. Why would they waste their time searching for her?

Jay stood up quickly, pushing the chair back so hard that it clattered to the floor. "I'm going to London."

"What? Jay—"

"I have to find her." Jay moved to door, and Shannon subtly stood in front of her to block her path.

"How are you going to do that, Jay? Drive around South London asking if any drug dealers took your sister?"

"I have to do something. I can't just sit here." Shannon went to Jay and pulled her into her arms. Jay buried her face in Shannon's neck and clung to her.

"It's okay, it's okay. They'll find her."

It probably wasn't true, but Jay needed to believe it. Before she could stop herself, she began to cry. Shannon just held her tighter and rocked her gently.

After a while, Jay sighed and straightened. She smiled at Shannon sheepishly. "Thanks for that."

"Anytime," Shannon replied softly, reaching out to wipe at the tears that were still wet on Jay's cheeks.

Jay caught her hand and kissed the palm. "I don't know what I'd have done without you here."

"You don't need to worry about that. I'm not going anywhere."

The meaning of the statement struck Jay with the force of its intent. *Isn't she going anywhere? Doesn't she need to go back to LA at some point? And if she decides to stay here, what does that mean for us?* Jay couldn't allow herself to hope that maybe this thing between them could go somewhere. There were too many obstacles, and Jay hadn't yet told Shannon her biggest secret.

There were too many questions, and now was not the time to be thinking about it all. First, they needed to get Kelly back. They could worry about the rest later.

Someone knocked on the door, and Jay jerked at the sound.

"I'll get it." Shannon went to the door.

Jay couldn't reply or react. She just stood woodenly, like she was waiting for axe to fall.

"Hello, madam. I'm sorry to bother you, but I have some news. Can I come in?" It was the tall policeman, the one who had been so kind earlier.

"Come in." Shannon came to stand by Jay and held her close.

"We've found Kelly. She's okay."

Jay felt the tension, which had her body coiled so tightly all evening, slowly dissipate, and she drew out a slow breath.

"Oh, thank Christ. Where is she? Can I see her? I want to—"

The policeman held up his hand to stem the flow of questions. "At the moment, she's helping us with our enquiries. We'll—"

"What the fuck are you talking about?" Jay snarled and made a move toward him before Shannon took hold of her arm and kept her in place.

"*Jay*. Let's listen to him."

The policeman cleared his throat and continued. "They took her to a council estate. She was fortunate that it was a couple of dealers at the bottom of the food chain who got hold of her. One of them got cold feet about the whole thing and phoned in a tip. I suppose he wasn't quite ready to make the leap from dealing a few pills to kidnapping. Your sister is helping us with our enquiries at the moment. She hasn't been charged with anything. *Yet*."

"What does that mean?" Jay felt Shannon hold on tighter to her.

"It means we won't be pressing any charges as long as she's assisting us. We're after them, not her."

"When can I see her?" Jay asked again through clenched teeth.

"Not until the morning. They'll interview her first thing. If she cooperates, there won't be any need to charge her."

"You're blackmailing her?" Shannon asked bluntly.

"I wouldn't call it that. The fact is, your sister is mixed up with some nasty people. If she hadn't robbed off of a couple of small timers...well, they probably would have just killed her."

Jay gave a jerk, and Shannon tightened her hold. "Please, let us have the details of where you're holding her. She's entitled to a lawyer, right?" Shannon said.

"She has a court-appointed—"

"Sir, please let me have the details of where you're holding her. We'd like her to have *our* lawyer present at her interrogation?"

After the officer left, Jay watched in wonder as Shannon got on the phone to her people, as she called them. Jay protested that she couldn't afford the kind of solicitor who worked for the firms Shannon's people were talking about.

Shannon waved her off like she was a pesky fly and continued with her mission to obtain the best representation she could get.

Jay almost laughed out loud at one point as she watched Shannon channel her inner diva. Finally, off the phone, she sat down at the table and took the cup of tea Jay offered her.

"Thanks. I need this."

"I think that I'm the one who should be thanking you. I have a bit of savings, so I can pay you back—"

Shannon waved her away again. "Jay, I have a lot of money. I'm not saying that to brag, but the truth is, this is a drop in the ocean, so don't worry about it. They've got a guy going down now. He won't be able to spring her tonight, but he'll kick up a huge stink about every question they ask her, and she'll be out in the morning, and we can bring her home."

"God, thank you so much." Jay looked at Shannon and was hit with a wave of something like love—*something like love? Of course it's love. You love her. You always have.*

Shannon was the anchor she needed to steady herself. It surprised her, that feeling, when for so many years she had relied only on herself. Shannon had stood by her through Kelly's recovery and helped to take care of all of them.

And she was still here, steady and calm and sure. Without meaning to, or even being fully aware of what she was doing, Jay reached out for her, and Shannon came into her arms without hesitation.

Jay held her close and breathed in the scent of her. She took strength from the solid warmth of her body.

"Thank you," Jay whispered against her ear.

Shannon didn't answer. Instead she pulled Jay tighter. Gently, she released her again, took her hand, and led her upstairs.

* * *

Shannon had only meant to lay down with Jay and sleep. She stripped to her underwear, and Jay had done the same. Before she knew what was happening, Jay moved towards her and pushed her leg gently between Shannon's. Her mouth lowered to Shannon's, probing, soft and sweet. Shannon's hands moved down to grip Jay's hips and pull her thigh tight against her own sex.

She sensed Jay needed this connection. If she was being honest, Shannon did too. It had been a hell of a night—a hell of a year—and Jay was Shannon's anchor. Sweet, kind Jay. Shannon didn't know what would happen between them, but she knew she loved her—had always loved her. And she didn't want to let her go again, no matter what sacrifices they would have to make to be together.

She heard Jay groan quietly. She deepened her kisses; her hips began to rock. Supporting herself on one arm, Jay stroked her other hand down Shannon's side, then back up again to cup her breast and rub her thumb over her hard nipple.

Soon, Jay's kisses became more urgent and demanding, Shannon's bra was unclipped and thrown to the side, her panties pulled down and off. She wasn't aware of Jay removing her own underwear until she felt her, hot and slick against her thigh. Then, Jay was going down, down, down, her mouth and tongue and lips teasing, sucking, licking, tasting.

Shannon bucked on the bed, grasped Jay's head between her hands, and urged her to go harder and faster. Her orgasm came quickly, battering her like a wave, obliterating all thought and feeling, until all she knew was Jay. And then Jay was crying.

"Are you okay?" Shannon whispered. She urged her upwards and into her arms. Jay came willingly and buried her face into Shannon's breast. "I'm just so..."

"I know." Shannon stroked her hair and held her close until she felt Jay's body soften and relax.

They stayed like that for a long time, and Shannon finally drifted off to sleep. Later, Jay shifted, and then she was holding Shannon and whispering words that she could hardly hear, but as sleep dragged her back down again, she thought she heard the word *love*.

* * *

Jay lay awake for a long time after Shannon had fallen asleep. She loved her. Of that she had no doubt, and she thought Shannon might love her back. Could it be that simple? That easy? She was used to fighting for what she wanted, and used to losing. And what about Shannon? Jay thought she wanted to be with her too. But that was now. She didn't know everything about Jay's past, or about what she had done. Shannon wouldn't want her after she found out—and even if she did, she certainly couldn't have her career *and* Jay. She would be tarred with the same brush, and no one would touch her.

Carefully, Jay disentangled herself from Shannon, trying not to wake her, and went downstairs.

CHAPTER NINE

"Where did you get off to last night?" Shannon pinched a piece of toast from Alfie's plate and sat at the kitchen table.

"Sorry, I couldn't sleep." Jay dipped some more egg onto the piece of toast and directed it at Alfie's mouth.

"You don't have to apologise. I just wondered if it was because of what happened with us."

"*No!* Please, Shannon, don't think that. Last night was great. I just..."

"I understand. I just wanted to make sure."

"They told us we could go to the police station at lunchtime. I asked Mrs Fritz to come and watch Alfie."

"Did you tell her what happened?"

Jay snorted. "She called *me*. It's the gossip of the century. Everyone wants to know about the police cars parked outside most of the night. It's a small village, but someone always sees something. Soon, they'll start making up what they don't know."

"Just like home. Listen, I have to go back to the cottage and get a change of clothes. Shall I meet you back here at eleven?"

"Okay, thanks. I'm really sorry about all of this."

"Jay, stop apologising. I'm glad I'm here."

"Why?" Jay looked genuinely confused.

"I care about you, you idiot. *That's* why." Shannon stood, kissed both Jay and Alfie on the head, and left.

As Jay was finishing up with Alfie, a knock sounded at the door. She checked her watch, thinking it was too early for Mrs Fritz. She stood, brushing the crumbs from her shirt, and went to answer it.

"Hello, dear." Mrs Fritz's eyes were bright, and Jay fancied that she could see her nose twitching with the scent of potential gossip in the air. "Is everything all right?"

"Fine, Mrs Fritz. Please, come in."

Mrs Fritz followed Jay into the house, her eyes darting about, no doubt looking for clues. Maybe bloodstains or bullet holes, Jay thought, smiling to herself.

"Thank you so much for doing this. It's a real help."

"No thanks necessary, dear. Always happy to help a neighbour."

"Well, it's very kind."

"Nonsense. Jay, dear. What happened last night? You know that I'm not one to gossip, but apparently you had a lot of police cars up here."

If it hadn't been for Shannon and Kelly, Jay would have been tempted to tell her, just to see the look on her face. "Not a lot, Mrs Fritz, just one." Jay turned to see her looking expectantly, and sighed. She supposed she would have to give her something. "I thought I saw someone down at Henry's, trying to break in."

"Oh Lord!" Mrs Fritz cried.

"It was a false alarm, Mrs Fritz. Everything is fine." Jay felt bad; she hadn't meant to scare the old woman. Maybe it was just as well that she hadn't mentioned the drug dealers kidnapping her sister.

"And Henry?"

"Fine, too," Jay quickly assured her. "Honestly, Mrs Fritz, it was just me overreacting. Please don't worry."

"Well, as long as everyone's okay."

Not yet, Jay thought. *But they will be. Soon.*

* * *

Shannon sat waiting in a hardback plastic chair. It was her second time in a police station, but her first in the UK, and she thought they seemed to be pretty much the same. The floor was painted a dull grey colour, and various posters were dotted about, showing pictures of wanted men and women whose expressions ranged from angry to bored. She'd studied them all briefly and decided she didn't know anyone. It was a shame really, as she'd calculated the reward money for information leading to their arrests would net her about seventy grand.

Shannon thought of Jay being somewhere like this all those years ago and how scared she must have been. Shannon wondered if she felt nervous about being back.

Jay had told her about the conversation with Mrs Fritz on the way here, and Shannon had been in fits of laughter. They'd talked casually, and Shannon had felt something settle between them. Something comfortable and easy. Last night, when she'd still been mostly asleep, she thought she'd heard Jay say she loved her. She tried not to think beyond that. Shannon had a sexy, kind woman who loved her, and the rest—all of the complications—could wait until later.

* * *

Jay sat on the hard plastic chair and faced the officer. She remembered this place well—not this particular station, of course, but they were all alike for the most part. Sterile walls, chairs just this side of uncomfortable, and the temperature just a little too cold. She shifted in her seat and took a deep breath. She had to keep reminding herself that this was not then. No one was going to lock her up or try to twist her words this time.

An image of Shannon formed in her mind's eye, and she was suddenly calm. She didn't want to think about what that meant. Only yesterday, she had decided to take the plunge, to see where this thing with Shannon went. To live in the moment for once. And now, was she changing her mind? Jay didn't think she'd ever been this confused in her life.

Since she'd moved here, her life had taken on a kind of comforting monotony. Sometimes she got lonely—well most of the time—and sometimes she'd thought about Shannon—well, all of the time.

Then, without warning, Shannon had come steaming back into her life, making her want things she couldn't have, and most of all, lean on somebody else for a change. Shannon had gladly and willingly been there for her through all of this—she was still here, sitting next to her and waiting for Kelly. She hadn't flinched from any of it, and Jay wondered about a person who had that kind of strength. She didn't have any right to ask Shannon to stay, to not leave her. And she would leave her, when she knew what Jay had done. Of course she would. How could she not? Being with Jay would ruin her career, because Jay was not who Shannon thought she was.

She turned her attention now to the officer in front of her. She would get this done, get Kelly home, and then see where things lay with Shannon.

* * *

When Jay walked into the family room, Kelly was perched on a sofa in the corner. She looked small and vulnerable, and Jay wanted to gather her up and take her home where she would never let her out of her sight again.

"Hey, Kel," she said softly, going to sit beside her. "I've come to take you home."

To her surprise, Kelly leaned into her and began to cry. "They aren't going to charge you. It's all right."

"I've made such a mess, Jay." Her voice came out strangled and raw. "Such a mess of everything."

"It's okay." Jay held her sister tight while she sobbed.

Eventually she quietened and leaned back in Jay's arms. "I want to go to rehab. I don't want to be like this anymore. I'm so tired. I want a life, like you're getting with Shannon."

Was that what she was doing? Was she finally putting the past behind her? She did feel less afraid, less lonely inside. She only hoped things wouldn't change when Shannon found out what she'd done.

It was time to tell her.

* * *

Jay pulled up outside the farm after dropping Shannon off to find a car sitting out front. She didn't recognise it. She sat for a moment, contemplating the idea of just driving away. What about Alfie? She sighed and got out, the gravel crunching beneath her feet as she made her way to the house.

"Hello, dear. I was just making some tea for Ms Stone. She's from social services," Mrs Fritz said quickly, as soon as Jay came through the door.

Social services. Great. Jay walked forward and held out her hand. "I'm Jay."

"Harriet. Pleased to meet you."

"I'll just go and check on Alfie, see if he's up yet." Mrs Fritz put down two cups of tea and went upstairs. Jay was surprised she was leaving before a conversation that was bound to be prime gossip fodder. *That's not fair. She's a gossip, but she's a good woman.* This was not something she would be happy to spread around the village.

"What can I do for you, Harriet?" Jay sipped her tea, doing her best to look relaxed. She wished Shannon were here.

"First of all, I'm sorry to have come without notifying you first."

"It's okay. Things have moved pretty quickly."

"Yes, they have. I'm so pleased to hear that Kelly has gone into rehab. I don't know if you're aware, but we've been involved with Alfie several times now."

"I imagine that you would have been. I dropped Kelly off this afternoon. Look, Harriet, so that we're clear, Alfie's staying with me. I'm more than able and willing to look after him."

"I'm sure, but it's not really that simple."

"Why's that?"

"Well, ordinarily, we would always place the child with family where possible."

"I'm his aunt."

"You have a conviction for murder."

"I did my time, and I've never been in any kind of trouble since. In fact, quite the opposite. I've built a business and a life—a good life. I can take care of him." Jay stopped, her tone close to begging, and she would beg if that was what it took to keep Alfie with her. She had no pride where he was concerned. Or Kelly for that matter. She needed Kelly to know that Alfie was with her, and not in some horrible children's home, or in foster care.

The other woman seemed to soften a little at that. "I'm not saying you wouldn't. Or even that we won't allow you to have custody. All I'm saying, is your situation makes things more complicated."

"What do we do? What do I have to do? Whatever it is, I'll do it."

* * *

After she had seen Harriet out, Jay went to the dresser and picked up a phone book. She had been putting this off, but it was time. She wasn't even sure if the number she had still worked. The last time she'd spoken to her mother was four years ago. It was short and awkward. Kelly had been in trouble again, and she was at her wits' end. She'd hoped her mother would help—would be able to do something that Jay had not been able to.

Just thinking about the conversation now made her gut clench. It was like talking to a stranger—which, Jay supposed, she was. After Jay went to prison, her mother had cut all contact with her. Kelly told her that she remarried several years into Jay's sentence, and when Kelly disappointed her too, she'd made a break from both of her daughters.

For the most part, Jay didn't think of her. They'd never been close, even when Jay was a child. She'd always been one for appearances, regardless of what was going on behind the scenes. Even at the end, when it had all come out, Jay could still hear the last thing she said to her as she was led away in handcuffs: *'Why did you have to bring this out in the open? Why couldn't you have just left things alone?'* Jay was stunned, and then furious. But she was Kelly's mother, and she should know what had happened.

The phone rang several times before it was picked up. "Hello?" A man's voice. Jay cleared her throat. "May I speak with Caroline, please?"

"Who shall I say is calling?"

"Jay. Her daughter." For a moment, Jay thought the man would hang up. He was silent for a while, and then she heard the sound of the receiver being placed on a table.

"Jay?" Her mother didn't sound pleased to hear from her. "I thought we agreed—"

"I wouldn't have called if it wasn't important." The sound of her mother's voice brought all the memories rushing back, and none of them were good. She heard her mother sigh on the other end of the line. "What's happened now? Honestly, I don't know what I did to deserve—"

"It's about Kelly. She got herself into some trouble—"

"Drugs again? Honestly, Jay, I really don't know why you're calling me about this."

"Mum, just listen. It's different this time. She's gone into rehab. I think she'd like to see you."

"What about the boy? Is he staying with you?"

"You mean your grandson? Alfie? Yes, he's staying with me."

"Good, because we really don't have the room."

Jay knew through Kelly the man she married was rich. Kelly told her he had a huge townhouse in Chelsea. It didn't matter. There was no way Jay would allow Alfie to live with her mother. "It's fine. I want him here. With me."

"Very well."

Jay noticed that her mother hadn't answered her question. "Will you visit her?"

"I don't know. Let me think about it, Jay."

"Fine, then. I'll call you—"

"No, I'll call you. Goodbye, Jay."

* * *

Shannon had offered to babysit Alfie while Jay was refereeing between her mother and sister.

She didn't expect Caroline to actually agree to visit Kelly in rehab, but she guessed there must still be a beating heart somewhere beneath all the hairspray and Chanel No. 5.

Kelly begged Jay to come too because she couldn't deal with being left alone with her. Jay didn't blame her.

They sat in the conservatory. It was almost like a hotel with its manicured lawns and tiny tea cups. Jay held one now as she sat in a wicker garden chair trying to keep the conversation going.

"Weather's nice for spring, isn't it?" she said, lamely.

Kelly rolled her eyes. "You must be desperate."

"Yes," Caroline said, ignoring Kelly's input, "my daffodils came up much earlier than I was expecting. What about your...I forget what you grow, Jay."

"Hops," Kelly supplied.

"Yes, hops. Did they come up early too?"

"They aren't like flowers, Mum. They don't just come up."

Jay laughed. "I didn't know you were an expert on hops, Kelly."

"I must have picked it up by osmosis one of the times you were droning on about them," Kelly shot back and winked.

"Girls, really. Let's try and be civil." Caroline glanced around to see who could hear them.

"We were only joking, Mum," Kelly said.

The next hour dragged by, and Jay could tell Kelly was as relieved as she was when their time was up.

Jay kissed Kelly goodbye and promised to come back in a few days. "Alone," Kelly hissed in her ear, and Jay laughed.

Not really expecting her to agree, Jay invited her mother back to the farm to see Alfie and meet Shannon. She was shocked when she agreed. Jay wondered how Shannon would take her. The thought made her chuckle.

* * *

"Jay tells me that you're an actress."

Jay watched as her mother studied Shannon in the way she had of assessing everyone, and usually finding them wanting in some way. She was certain Caroline knew who Shannon was.

"Yes, I am," said Shannon. "And what do you do, Caroline?" Shannon matched her mother with a cool, appraising gaze of her own.

"Oh, I'm on a number of committees and boards in London." Caroline waved her hand dismissively. "My step-daughter is an actress, you know. Perhaps you've heard of her? Camilla Bowen-Hall?"

"I'm afraid not."

"No, well, she's just starting out really. She's had a number of good reviews for a play she's been doing in London. Shakespeare." Caroline said the word *Shakespeare* as though it were an incantation. "But, she's more of a classical actress. I understand you're in Hollywood."

Shannon ignored the obvious slight; she'd been up against worse than Caroline. "Yep, I just make plain old blockbusters."

Jay laughed, and then quickly tried to hide it with a cough. "Mum, I was going to show you the hops. They're coming along really well. Did you want to—"

"I'm afraid I should get back, Jay. It's quite a long drive to London, and I don't like doing it in the dark."

"Okay then." Jay didn't know why she was hurt. She was used to her mother. She was surprised she even agreed to come back to the house at all. But then, she was all about appearances, even in front of people she considered beneath her, as she plainly did with Shannon.

"Did you want to say goodbye to Alfie?" Jay asked.

"No, I don't think that's necessary, Jay. Take care."

"I will." She didn't say 'see you soon,' or 'I'll call.' She wasn't welcome in her mother's life—hadn't been for a very long time. For the first time, she didn't mind so much. She didn't know if it was because of Shannon, or Alfie, or the way everyone in the village had rallied round her. Either way, for the first time she could remember, Jay didn't feel so lonely. And now, it was time to tell Shannon the truth. All of it. She just hoped it wouldn't be the end of them.

Chapter Ten

Jay sat facing Shannon on the sofa. She was unsure what to say or how to begin, and she was scared. Scared about Shannon's reaction and inevitable rejection. She owed her the truth. She should have told her a long time ago, and she couldn't put it off any longer.

"I always find the best place to start is the beginning," Shannon said quietly. She squeezed Jay's hand and gave her a kind smile.

Jay nodded and cleared her throat. "I told you about my father? That he died?"

"Yes, when you were three or so?"

"Right. My mother—Caroline—remarried when I was ten. Kelly was six. Her new husband was rich—all her husbands are."

"How many times has she been married?"

"Four, I think."

"She must like weddings." Shannon grinned.

"God, she must. I was only invited to one. The second one. Kelly and I didn't even know she met someone until a week before when she said she was getting married and we were moving the countryside."

"Forgive me for saying this, Jay. Your mother is a bitch."

"She probably wouldn't win Mother of the Year," Jay agreed.

"What happened next?"

"Not a lot. She married him—David. I really got on well with him. His house was great, lots of land. He used to take me shooting at weekends—not animals, though he did do that. I liked the clay pigeon shooting. I couldn't bring myself to kill the animals."

Shannon reached out and took Jay's hand. "That doesn't surprise me. You're very gentle."

"No, I'm not. Wait until you hear the rest of it." Jay's voice took on a bitterness she couldn't keep out. She tried to pull her hand out of Shannon's, but Shannon just held it tighter.

"David took me pretty much everywhere. I was the child he'd never had. We both loved the outdoors. He reminded me of my dad in so many ways. David loved the idea of farming hops. He was interested when I told him about my grandparents' farm and how I planned to go into the same business. He even offered to set me up with a place of my own. The plan was I'd do an agricultural degree, and then he'd purchase some land for me. We would be partners."

"He sounds like a nice guy."

"I thought so. I know you'd never think it, but before, in London, Kelly was the one who was good in school. She always got good grades, was in the school sports teams. I was the one that caused my mother some problems. Not big ones, just stuff like not paying attention, not doing my homework. I got in with the naughty kids."

Jay remembered Kelly as a happy and popular student. How things could change.

"When we moved in with David, it pretty much reversed. Kelly was getting into trouble, and I was doing well—I had something to aim for, you see. When she was about thirteen, she started drinking and smoking and bunking off school. I should have questioned her about it, but I was so wrapped up in my own life. I barely noticed."

"You were a kid yourself. I don't understand why you'd think that you were to blame for Kelly's behaviour."

Jay looked at Shannon, whose eyes were soft and full of understanding. *Let's see how understanding she is by the end.* "Wait until you hear the rest of it."

"I don't think anything you say will make me feel differently about you," Shannon said.

"I came home from school early one day. I was in the middle of my last exams before university." Jay fixed her eyes somewhere beyond Shannon. She couldn't face her. "I saw Kelly's bag in the hall. I knew she was home when she should have been at school. I went upstairs to give her a bollocking. I didn't knock. I just...I walked in. I saw them. I saw *him.*" Jay turned abruptly and pulled her hand from Shannon's. She scrubbed her face roughly, trying to rub the memory away, but it was still there. Fresh as the day it happened.

"It's okay, Jay. Tell me." Shannon moved closer and stroked Jay's back in circles.

"He was raping her. He'd been doing it for years, and I had no idea. How could I have been so blind?"

Shannon didn't say anything—what could she say? Jay half expected her to stand up and leave. Instead, Shannon squeezed her shoulder. She continued with the slow circles on Jay's back.

"What happened next, baby?"

"He had a gun safe in his study. He'd showed me where he kept the key. I swear to God, Shannon, I just wanted to scare him—make him leave her alone."

Jay remembered it clearly. She remembered going to the safe, holding the gun in her hands, how heavy and powerful it felt.

"By the time I got back to Kelly's room, he had got out of the bed and put on his underwear. He was standing there like he'd done nothing wrong. Like *I* should be the one ashamed for walking in on them. I pointed it—the gun—I pointed it at him. And he...looked annoyed. *Just annoyed.*"

David had stood there in his boxers, hands on his hips. *'Jay, you're being ridiculous. Put the gun down. This is silly.'*

"I was so angry. I don't think I wanted to shoot him. But, he came toward me—fast. He had his hands out as if he was going to take the gun. So, I...I shot him."

She remembered how he had crumpled like a paper doll. This big man. Her friend. "I kept shooting over and over again. Kelly was screaming. The gun was a double-barrelled shotgun, so I only could have shot him twice, but I just kept pulling the trigger even though the gun was empty." Jay looked up at Shannon feeling bewildered. Even after all these years, she still couldn't understand how it happened. "I really didn't mean to shoot him...but...I couldn't stop."

"It's okay." Shannon pulled Jay to her, and Jay rested against her shoulder.

"Everything was a blur after that. The police came—I still don't know who called them. I was arrested. It moved quickly—the trial. They told me if I pleaded guilty, I'd get seven years. Kelly told them everything, how it had been going on pretty much as soon as we went to live with him. She saved me from a much longer sentence."

"You didn't deserve a long sentence."

"I killed somebody." Jay pulled away. "It doesn't matter why I did it; I had no right to take someone's life."

"No, you didn't. But, he was raping your sister. We reap what we sow, and he reaped a lot of bad karma."

* * *

Shannon couldn't blame Jay for what she did. In that situation, she thought she would have done the same thing. She wasn't proud of herself—you were supposed to turn the other cheek, right?

All the same, Shannon felt David got what he deserved. Her only regret was Jay had to be the one to do it. To a man she had obviously loved, and who had betrayed both her and Kelly in the worst possible way.

"My mother refused to have anything to do with me. She took Kelly and moved back to London—went back to her maiden name, as the story was all over the papers. Kelly came to see me once. But...it was too hard for her. I thought she blamed me. She told me recently it was because she felt so ashamed."

"It wasn't her fault. It wasn't your fault either. It was *his* fault and only his."

"You don't hate me?"

Shannon wanted to cry at the look of uncertainty in Jay's eyes.

"*No!* God, no, I don't hate you. How could you think I ever would? Jay, I love you." She didn't have time to stop the words before they popped out of her mouth. *Did she love her?* She thought that she did—was sure of it. She'd loved her ten years ago, too.

"You mustn't. Shannon, if people find out that you're with me...they'll find out about David, and then your career will be ruined." Jay took Shannon's hands.

"Why don't you let me worry about that? Besides, I've done a pretty good job of ruining my career all by myself."

"Shannon—"

"Jay. I don't need protection from you."

"But—"

Shannon silenced her with a kiss. As it began to deepen, Shannon pulled away breathlessly. "Take me upstairs."

"Shannon, I don't think—"

"Will you just shut up? You're getting on my nerves."

Jay laughed, holding up her hands. "You've convinced me. I'll need to be really unromantic and check on Alfie first though."

Shannon laughed. "Sure. How's he taking to his new room?"

Jay grinned. "There's a car bed in there so he loves it. Come on."

* * *

Back in her own bedroom, Jay rested her head on her hand. With the other, she slowly stroked Shannon. The backs of her fingers, tracing the angles and planes of soft, smooth skin. She looked at her, this beautiful woman who said she loved her, and she couldn't quite believe it. What had she done to deserve someone like Shannon?

Jay dipped her head and dropped kisses along Shannon's collarbone, the valley between her breasts. She made her way down the insides of her thighs, and then to her knees. She drew Shannon's leg upwards and kissed her exposed calf, then her ankle.

This is what it feels like to make love. Over the years, Jay had had all kinds of sex. Slow sex, fast sex, angry sex, sex where they'd spent more time laughing then actually doing it. This was new. She remembered when they'd met the first time, how she'd tried to make love to Shannon almost without meaning to. Shannon had pulled away, and Jay had been relieved. Not now. Now she wanted to make love to Shannon and show her how much she meant. That she loved her.

Jay used her mouth and her hands to show Shannon. She filled her up so there was no room for anything else. Jay took pleasure and gave it.

Shannon cried out as she came and reached for Jay. Jay moved up beside her. She pulled Shannon close and kissed her hair, her eyelids. Jay whispered that she loved her, and she meant it. She'd never loved anyone like she loved Shannon.

Jay woke a while later to find Shannon had moved down between her legs.

"Jesus." Jay hissed as Shannon's tongue began a slow exploration of her. Her tongue circled her clit, slowly at first, and then with more urgency as Jay couldn't help but grind her hips. As her orgasm began to build, Shannon started to suck. Her tongue rubbed against the tip of Jay's clit.

"Oh, Shannon, yes. Like that," Jay whispered, her hands cupping Shannon's head, urging her to go faster.

Shannon sucked harder, and Jay began to pump her hips. "I'm going to come." Then she did. A great wave crashed into her, over her and all the way through her. She cried out. Her body stiffened; every muscle vibrated.

Jay collapsed back onto the bed with a sigh, and Shannon made her way back up, trailing soft kisses over her abdomen, her chest, her neck, and finally her lips.

"Okay?" Shannon asked as she curled herself into Jay's side. Her head came to rest on Jay's chest.

"Yes," Jay replied weakly and wrapped her arm around Shannon. "Wow."

* * *

They stayed that way for a while, just holding each other. Then, Jay rolled over onto Shannon, taking the weight on her arms.

"Hey," she said.

"Hey, yourself." Shannon parted her legs so that Jay could lie between them.

Slowly, Jay lowered her head and kissed Shannon deeply before dipping her tongue into Shannon's mouth and running it along her bottom lip.

Shannon caught it between her lips and sucked, and Jay moaned. Releasing her, Shannon closed her eyes as Jay began to kiss her neck. They were slow, gentle kisses that started a warm glow low in her belly. Jay's fingers stroked her abdomen, and as she took a nipple in her mouth, Shannon moaned, the sensation shooting down into her clit. Jay began to suck gently, brushing her tongue over the nipple in a circular motion that made Shannon gasp.

"Harder, do it harder," Shannon moaned, and Jay did as she was told, taking most of Shannon's breast into her mouth and sucking hard. Her fingers travelled downwards, past Shannon's stomach, and brushed between her lips, lightly stroking her clit. Shannon raised her hips and pushed against Jay's fingers as they slid along her clit and then inside her. Shannon moaned.

She pushed down hard but felt her orgasm slither just out of reach as Jay's fingers gentled inside her. Jay stopped, and Shannon opened her eyes. "Jay, that isn't fair. Finish me."

Jay grinned. "Relax, I just want to taste you." She moved down on the bed and took Shannon in her mouth.

She used her tongue to make long, slow strokes over Shannon's clit. Shannon felt heavy and swollen. She decided to take things into her own hands and grabbed Jay's head, twisting her fingers in Jay's hair. "If you stop this time, I'm going to kill you."

Rather than answer, Jay smiled up at her. She began to rub her tongue lightly against the tip of Shannon's clit. Shannon felt her finger slip inside, hover at her entrance where the sensitive nerves were. Jay swirled her finger around and in and out gently before going up and hooking round to rub her G spot.

When Jay added her mouth to the mix, Shannon was pushed over the edge and into a powerful orgasm. She arched her back, and her hands reflexively dragged Jay's head against her centre.

She cried out as wave after wave crashed over her and pulled her under, until she lay still. She tried to catch her breath.

"Okay, time out." Shannon held up her hands and made a weak T sign.

"I think I have some electrolytes somewhere," Jay joked.

"Cake. I want cake."

"The one my mother brought with her?"

"Yeah, that'll do. Why did she bring you a cake?"

"She thinks it's the height of politeness."

"She wouldn't, if she knew I was eating it after having my way with her daughter."

Jay burst out laughing. "Is that what happened?"

"Yep. What are you still doing here, Jay? Go get me the damn cake." Shannon threw a pillow at Jay, who couldn't duck in time.

"You're grumpy when you're hungry."

"I don't see your legs moving, Jay."

Jay laughed again and got up.

* * *

"Tell me something about yourself." Jay licked cake from her fingers.

"What do you want to know?"

"Something no one else knows."

Jay and Shannon were propped against the headboard, eating cake with their fingers.

"Something no one else knows? Does it count if my mom knows?"

"That's fine."

"I told you I lived on a horse farm, right?"

"Yes."

"Well, we used to have to take the bus to school. We were the first to get picked up and the last to get dropped off. We lived so far from town that it would take, like, an hour to get home—you want that last bit of cake?"

"No, you have it. I'm full." Jay put the plate aside and pulled Shannon against her.

"Well, this one time, we were on the way back, and I really needed the bathroom. Like, I was about to shit my pants."

"Lovely."

"I'd made the mistake of telling my brother how bad I needed to go. Obviously, he's being totally obnoxious on the bus, which is making things worse. As soon as the bus pulls up, I jump off that fucking thing, and I start *running*. I mean, I'm on the edge."

"How old were you?"

"I think around eleven. Too old to shit my pants. So, my brother's running behind me, laughing, and then I get to the porch, like, I really thought I'd made it."

"Oh no."

"Yep. I totally shat my pants. It was horrible. If that isn't bad enough, my brother ran into the house shouting, 'Mom, Mom, Shannon crapped her pants.' I was mortified."

"At least it was just your mom and brother."

"Oh, no. See, my mom hosted this monthly book club—"

"Oh shit."

"Yeah."

"I love your shit and vomit stories."

"Good, I have a lot. When I tell them on talk shows, they cut them."

"Can't imagine why."

Shannon elbowed Jay playfully, then sat up. She put her hands around the back of Jay's head and held them there, tangling her fingers in Jay's hair.

She caught Jay's tongue between her lips and sucked it, eliciting a low moan from Jay. Shannon was suddenly wet and heavy. Jay pushed her backwards onto the bed; her long, lean body covered Shannon. Shannon parted her legs so Jay could slip between them.

Slowly, Jay started to grind against her. Jay broke the kiss and put her lips on Shannon's neck where she began to suck and nibble.

Shannon lifted her hips and moved in time with Jay. Jay slid her hand down to Shannon's crotch and began to rub her palm of her between Shannon's legs. Shannon moaned and ground herself against Jay's hand. "Oh yes, oh yes," she breathed.

Shannon shivered when Jay brushed her fingers over the soft pubic hair covering Shannon's sex.

Shannon swallowed hard, and her breathing became shallow. Her body was on fire.

"Put your fingers inside me. I need your fingers in me," Shannon whispered against Jay's ear. "Please, Jay, Jesus." Shannon groaned.

Jay smiled down at her. "How much do you want it?" she whispered.

Shannon's eyes fluttered open, hazy with lust, and she smiled lazily. "Oh I see. I would never have pegged you for a dirty talker."

Jay smiled in return, then pushed her finger into Shannon just a tiny bit.

"Oh." Shannon sighed.

"Tell me," Jay urged.

"I want your fingers in me. I want you to fuck me. Can't you feel how wet I am?" Shannon pushed her hips down, and the finger waiting just inside her entrance slipped inside farther.

* * *

"Oh, God."

Now it was Jay's turn to groan. She covered Shannon's mouth with her own and kissed her hard enough to bruise both their lips.

She pushed two fingers into Shannon and began to fuck her, the teasing was done with. Shannon tightened around her, rode her fingers hard. Her hips bucked, and she opened her legs wide.

"Oh yes. That's so good. Harder, Jay. Please, harder. Fuck me," she cried.

Jay did as she asked and slipped in a third finger. She pumped in and out of Shannon as hard and as fast as she could, her thumb pushing on Shannon's clit, until Shannon exploded underneath her, fingers digging into Jay's back as she cried out.

Breathing hard, Jay rolled onto her back, pulled Shannon on top of her, and held her, stroking her hair. After a minute, she asked, "Okay?"

"Yes. I'm great. Jesus." Shannon laughed.

"Good. That was awesome."

"I think it was more awesome for me," Shannon joked.

"No, me too. You feel amazing inside."

"Jay, what I said earlier...I meant it."

"The shit story?"

"You asshole. You know what I mean."

"Say it." Jay smiled. For the first time in as long as she could remember, she felt happy. Lighter.

"*Fine*. I love you."

"I love you too."

"Glad we got that sorted."

"Me too. Want to go again?"

"You're so romantic. I want to go to sleep. Ask me again tomorrow."

* * *

The first thing Jay heard when she woke was Alfie laughing. She smiled, thinking Shannon must have been playing with him. She was glad she had told Shannon her secret, and grateful beyond belief Shannon loved her in spite of what she'd done. *Shannon loves me.* Jay grinned to herself, got up, and headed downstairs.

Alfie was in his booster chair while Shannon attempted to wipe cereal from around his face. Somehow, it had ended up pretty much everywhere except in his mouth. She pulled a gloopy lump out of his hair.

"He got it down his back yesterday. *Under* his t-shirt" Jay came and sat beside them.

"It's driving me crazy." She turned and kissed Jay. "Good morning."

"Morning. Want me to take over?"

"Thanks. It's pretty much just his hands left to clean."

"Might be quicker to chuck him in the bath and hose him down."

Shannon laughed and passed Jay the cloth. "You may be right. I'll make coffee."

"Did you have any plans today?" Jay called over her shoulder.

Shannon spooned instant coffee into mugs. "You really need to buy better coffee. This is just bean ashes. No plans. Why?"

"I have to go to the village this morning. After that, I thought we might go out for the day. Maybe the beach? Alfie hasn't been before."

"It isn't too cold?"

Jay carefully wiped his chubby fingers, and Alfie giggled. "Should be okay. It's supposed to get quite warm for spring. There's plenty of places to go inside if it's too cold."

"Okay. I need to stop at the cottage for a change of clothes."

* * *

The bell tinkled over the door of the post office as Jay entered. Sarah smiled at her from behind the counter. "Hi, Jay. How are you?"

"I'm okay. You?"

"I'm well. Here's your post." She handed over a small stack of envelopes tied together with a rubber band. "Before I forget, Mrs Mackay was looking for you. Asked you to stop by the shop."

"No problem, thanks." Jay took the letters and left, wondering what Mrs Mackay needed to talk to her about.

She headed in the direction of the shop when Mrs Mackay hurried over, waving to her.

"Jay." Mrs Mackay was a little out of breath.

"Is everything okay?"

"I'm not sure. I was going to head up to your place, when I saw your truck just now."

Jay frowned. "What's wrong?"

"I don't know that anything is wrong, dear. I had a man in the shop earlier. Ratty little person, asking questions about you and your sister."

Jay's heart began beat faster. *Could it be Kelly's druggie boyfriend?* No, he would probably be laying low at the moment. "What did he look like?"

"Ratty. And nosy. I sent him away with a flea in his ear. I wanted you to know. He was at George Poole's as well—asking questions. I took a picture of him with that smartphone my granddaughter bought me for Christmas. Here."

Mrs MacKay held up the phone, and Jay looked at the photo. She was relieved to see it wasn't Kelly's ex, but the whole thing unnerved her all the same. Who was he?

"Thank you, Mrs Mackay. I appreciate you telling me."

"No bother, dear. Just be careful. I'll let you know if he comes sniffing around again."

Jay climbed into the Jeep as Mrs Mackay went back to her shop.

"What was that about?" Shannon asked.

"I'm not sure. Apparently somebody has been asking around about me and Kelly."

"Here? In the village?" Shannon sat up a little straighter. A bad feeling took shape in her gut. "Who would do that?"

"I really don't know."

"Maybe it's about me?"

Jay started the Jeep. "Maybe. Look, there's no point worrying about it." She forced a note of levity into her voice. Levity she didn't feel. Someone was asking questions about her, and that couldn't mean anything good. She reached across the seat and squeezed Shannon's thigh. "Let's go to the beach."

"Beach, beach!" cheered Alfie, making it sound more like 'bitch.'

* * *

Although it was warm for this time of year, the wind blowing in from the ocean was chilly. Alfie collected seashells, which had terrified him at first, until Jay explained the creatures didn't live in them anymore.

Joe came with them and was busy running in and out of the water, he barked each time a wave caught him.

"Will Alfie be able to stay with you?" Shannon asked.

"Hopefully. Until Kelly's better. I had a visit from social services a few days ago."

"Alfie belongs with *you*."

Jay smiled at Shannon's conviction. "It's complicated because of my criminal record. Hopefully, once I've jumped through a few hoops for them..."

"You'll be fine, Jay. Anyone who's seen you with him knows he should stay with you."

"Thank you." Jay leaned forward and kissed her. It felt nice to be able to do that. Jay still couldn't quite believe Shannon wanted to be with her. She'd promised herself not to analyse it too deeply. Her mind kept going back to her conversation with Mrs Mackay earlier. Could it be a reporter, after news about Shannon? If so, why would they want to know about Jay and Kelly?

During her sentence, Jay had had several offers from true crime writers and the like. They'd wanted interviews for their books or documentaries. Eventually they had faded away when new and more awful crimes were committed.

It was possible someone decided to bring it all up again, but why? Most people wouldn't remember the crime, so it didn't really make sense. *Just forget about it. Enjoy the day.*

Jay took Shannon's hand and squeezed. They were interrupted by the shrill sound of Shannon's mobile phone.

"Sorry," she said, hitting the green button. "Hello? ...Corin? Is that you? ...Corin, I can't hear you, the line is bad... Corin? ...Hello?"

"Everything okay?" Jay asked as Shannon put the phone away.

"I don't know. The line was really bad. I think she's done something though."

"What do you mean?" Jay's stomach dropped.

"I don't know. It was garbled, but I think I heard her say 'sorry.'"

"Why would she be sorry?"

"I don't think I really want to know. Come on, I don't want to discuss it now. Let's just have a nice day."

They did. Jay bought them all fish and chips on the pier. She took Shannon to the arcades, and they played the penny slots. Alfie wanted to ride the carousel over and over, until he felt sick. They ate donuts, candy floss, and had their picture taken in one of those cartoon cut-outs where someone would put their head through the hole and become a Victorian baby in a pushchair, or a strongman.

* * *

They were on their way back to the Jeep when Shannon's phone rang again. "Hello? Bethy?"

"Jesus, Shannon, where have you been? I've been trying to get in touch with you all day." Bethany sounded frantic and stressed.

"Sorry, the reception sucks here. What's up?" Shannon thought she knew.

"It's Corin. Honey, I'm so sorry. She sold you out. It's all over the Internet. You made front page on a couple of newspapers too."

Strangely enough, Shannon didn't feel anything. No—that wasn't true, she felt...relieved. "It's finally out."

"Looks like it. You don't sound too worried."

"I don't think I am." And, surprisingly, she really wasn't. "How bad was it?"

"It's Corin, Shannon."

"So...bad?"

"Actually, considering it was Corin, it could have been much worse."

"Well, it's done now, I guess."

Bethy blew out a breath on the other end of the line. "The thing is, there's a photograph of you. It's pretty grainy, but they have a shot of you with a woman. Kissing."

"Damn. The woman would be Jay." And that would be enough to send her running for the hills.

"I figured it might be. You should tell her. It's not going to be pretty. Maybe think about coming back to the States?"

Shannon looked over to see Jay motioning that she was going to put Alfie in the car.

"Look, Bethy, I have to go. I'll call you in a while."

"Sure. But, Shannon? Think about it. You're staying in a tiny village. You won't be able to hide when they find out where you are."

"You think Corin told them?"

"I don't know. Probably. You okay?"

"You know, I really am. I have to go, Bethy."

"Sure, okay. Call me?"

"I will. Promise." Shannon said goodbye and climbed into the Jeep.

"Everything okay?" Jay looked across at her and squeezed her thigh.

"Corin just outed me."

"That fu—" Jay looked quickly behind at Alfie, who was dozing, then continued in a whisper. "That fucking arsehole. What are you going to do?"

"Not a lot. I need to call my publicist when we get back. She's got to be having a coronary by now."

Jay nodded and started the Jeep. As they pulled away, Shannon reached across and stroked the back of her neck. "They have a photograph."

"Of us?" Jay's voice was flat.

"I think so."

"Jesus Christ."

By the time they got back to the village, the sun had mostly set. Jay was quiet most of the drive back, and Shannon wondered if she was thinking up her goodbyes.

She was skittish anyway—always had been. This might just be enough to push her away completely. Shannon knew she had created this isolated and lonely life for herself for a reason.

* * *

They pulled up at the farm, and so far, so good. Jay was half expecting reporters to be camped outside with their cameras and microphones. She got Alfie out from his car seat and carried him inside.

Jay knew Shannon was worried about how she would take this. The truth was, Jay wasn't sure what to do. She had carefully constructed this life for herself. It was sometimes lonely, but it was quiet, and there was comfort in that. Risking it wouldn't be the reason she would give Shannon up.

Jay knew it wouldn't be long before everyone learned who she was and what she had done. Once that happened, Shannon's career would be over. Maybe Shannon didn't care now.

But in time she would. It would come between them, and she would rather let Shannon go than have her hate her. They would be hounded wherever they went, lurid stories in the tabloids; people that Jay had gone to school with would all sell stories about how she'd killed small animals as a kid, or some other equally sensational crap. They would make up lies about them, until neither she nor Shannon would know what the truth was.

Jay had been a fool to believe this wouldn't happen. She was a fool to allow things to have gone this far.

Regardless of what Shannon thought, it was Jay who had made the decision all those years ago that set her on this course. She would not take Shannon down with her.

* * *

Jay went upstairs to put Alfie to bed and take a shower. She said it would give Shannon privacy to make her calls. Shannon thought she wanted to hide out. She knew Jay well enough to know she was panicking. Shannon had seen the gears turning in her head all the way back.

"Hello, Carla?"

"Jesus, fuck, Shannon! I've been trying to get a hold of you all fucking day."

"I was at the beach. There wasn't a good service."

"Oh, you were at the beach? The *beach*? Well, I hope you had a nice time, because all hell's been breaking loose here."

Carla sounded like she was about to have a heart attack. Shannon could see her publicist's face now, probably the same one she'd had when Shannon face-planted into the backdrop at that awards thing. "Is it bad?"

"Bad? Is it *bad*? Yes, it's fucking bad. Your girlfriend sold her story to the worst, most vicious, gossip rag in the world. And the editor is that bitch we sued a couple years back. I'll bet she's just thrilled to be able to break this story."

"Oh."

"That's it? 'Oh'?"

"What do you want me to say? I didn't know she was going to do it." Shannon rubbed at her temples where the first throb of a headache was beginning to build.

Carla sighed on the other end of the line. "I know you didn't, honey. But it's really bad. We need to do some serious damage limitation. And for that, you need to be back here. When can you get a flight out?"

"Give me a couple days." Shannon didn't want to go. It was just like last time. She would be leaving Jay again. With time and distance, Jay would probably convince herself it was for the best, and Shannon would never hear from her again. Her heart hurt at the thought of it. She couldn't leave her again.

"You can't get anything sooner?"

"I have some things to tie up here first."

"That woman in the picture?" Carla guessed.

"I love her."

"Oh, Jesus! Shannon, I do not want to hear that from you. Okay? Do you understand?"

"Carla, I won't lie about her or about myself anymore. I'm done pretending to be something I'm not."

"Shannon, I'm begging here. Do not do *anything* until I talk to you. Okay? Honey?"

"Fine. As long as you know I won't change my mind."

Carla ignored her. "Let me know your flight details, and I'll have someone pick you up. If anything happens, *anything at all*, call me. I'll fly over. Do *not* talk to anyone."

"Fine." Shannon hung up and turned to see Jay standing behind her. Jay opened her mouth to speak, but Shannon cut her off—she knew what she was going to say. "Don't, Jay. Don't."

"Shannon—" Jay walked towards her with hands upturned.

"No. I have to go back and fix this. Then, I'm flying right back here. I'm not leaving you. Not this time. And you'd better not be thinking of leaving me."

Jay nodded. "Let's just watch a film, okay? We'll snuggle up on the sofa and watch a film."

"Okay."

* * *

At first, Jay thought it was lightning. White light blasted behind her eyes—one, two times. She realised she and Shannon had fallen asleep on the sofa, and it was not lightning. It was a flashbulb from a camera, outside the windows. She was grateful they had drawn the curtains.

She heard voices outside and checked her watch to see it was just after eight in the evening.

"Shannon, wake up." She shook her gently, and Shannon came awake groggily.

"What's going on?"

Jay nodded to the window. "I think they're here. Outside. You should call your publicist."

"What the fuck? How do you know?" Shannon jumped up and went to the window. As she reached out to pull back the curtain, Jay grabbed her hand. "No, Shannon. Don't. They're right outside."

"They can't fucking do this!" Shannon cried, her eyes glittered with anger.

"I know. They're trespassing." Jay walked away.

"What are you going to do?"

Shannon's voice was small and uncertain.

"Tell them to get off my fucking land."

"No, Jay, don't. Stay inside. I'll call Carla. She can send—"

"It's *my* land, Shannon. I won't stand for it."

"Jay, don't do anything stupid. Please."

"Don't worry, I'm not going to shoot anybody."

"That's not what I—"

Shannon's words were lost as Jay slammed the front door behind her.

* * *

It's a fucking circus. Jay walked out into a flashbulb party. Voices shouted questions from all directions, and she suddenly had a glimpse into Shannon's life. *No wonder she puts up walls. How can she deal with this?* Jay did her best to shield her eyes from the cameras.

* * *

"She's *what*? Why did you let her go out there?" Carla screamed, and Shannon held the phone away from her ear.

"It's not like I could stop her. Plus, they are trespassing."

"This just gets better and better. Shannon, *do not go outside.*"

"I wasn't planning to."

"I'm sending a car for you now. Go directly to the airport. *Do not speak to anyone.*"

"Fine." What else could she do?

Alfie was upstairs asleep, and she couldn't have this around him. She knew the paparazzi, and she knew they would camp out there forever if they needed to. If she left, they would follow, and Jay and Alfie would be left alone.

It was the right thing to do, but her heart ached. *Jay will never forgive me for bringing this to her door.* Shannon had seen her face. Her anger was palpable, and Shannon had caused it.

Jay had built herself this safe place, this quiet place, and Shannon had steamrolled in and destroyed it. She closed her eyes. *Please don't hate me, Jay.*

"Shannon? Hello? Shannon, are you still there?"

"Yes. Don't worry. I'll stay here and wait for the car. I won't speak to anyone."

* * *

"Is it true you're in a lesbian relationship with Shannon Dempsey...?"

"Did you really murder your stepfather...?"

"Does Shannon know you're a killer...?"

Jay turned her head back and forth as the questions were fired at her from all directions. She recognised one man as the person Mrs MacKay had taken a picture of earlier. He was a fucking reporter.

Cameras flashed, blinding her, and all at once she couldn't breathe. *I can't do this.*

"You're trespassing on private property." She shouted to be heard above the reporters. "You have five minutes to leave. After that I'm calling the police."

No one seemed to be listening to her. They continued to call out questions. *Now what?* She had no shotgun to fire into the air—and wouldn't they just bloody love that? *Convicted murderer shoots at reporters.*

Jay turned and went back into the house to call the police.

* * *

"Jay?"

Jay turned at the sound of Shannon's voice, and the sight of her, so angry and hurt, twisted Shannon's gut.

"I need to call the police. They won't leave." Jay strode past her to the phone.

"A car is coming for me soon. They'll leave then," Shannon said quietly. She wanted to go to Jay, but wasn't sure if she was welcome.

"I need to call the police," Jay said as if she hadn't heard her.

Shannon's heart clutched at the sight of the stranger before her. *She's going to leave me.*

"Jay."

Jay spun quickly, and there was fury in her eyes, "*What?* What, Shannon?"

Shannon recoiled as if struck. Jay was furious, and she was the cause. Her carefully constructed world was coming apart, and all because of Shannon.

"I...I'm sorry. I didn't mean..." Jay moved towards her, arms out.

"I know." Shannon stepped back, not wanting the contact. It would only make what Jay was going to do next harder.

"They know about me. About what I did. I'm so sorry." Jay hung her head.

"It's not your fault, Jay."

"This will ruin your career. You can deny we had a...you know..."

"Not really. We had a what, Jay? What was it that we had?" The sick feeling in her stomach was growing. Jay remained silent, and Shannon felt the need to fill the silence. *Don't you dare do this to me.* "It'll blow over in a few weeks. Trust me, they'll find someone else to hound."

"No, Shannon." Jay looked at her, and Shannon saw the finality in her eyes.

"Oh, you fucking coward."

"I'm sorry."

The misery in Jay's eyes only made Shannon angrier. "You're sorry. Of course you are. You are such a coward. You just keep on running, don't you?"

"Shannon, it's not about that. I—"

"Save it! I don't want to hear it. I am so sick of people telling me they're sorry. You aren't damn sorry at all. You liked the idea of fucking a movie star, didn't you?"

"*No!*"

"*Yes!* And now that it's all gotten a little real, you want to take it back." Shannon could see each cruel word cutting through Jay, but she couldn't stop. And the sick thing was, she knew none of it was true. She was so mad, and hurt, and she wanted to make Jay bleed too.

"Shannon, that isn't it. Please, just listen to me—"

"Fuck you, Jay." As she spat the words, she saw headlights turn into the courtyard and knew her car was here. *Must have broken every speed limit in the county.* Or, more likely, Carla already had them close by.

"Shannon, please don't go like this." Jay reached out her hand.

"*Don't fucking touch me!*" Shannon heard herself, and cringed inwardly. *Oh God, what am I doing to this woman?* She ran for the front door, pulled it open, and ran out into the night.

* * *

Jay watched her go. The flashbulbs started up again, and reporters shouted questions they had no right to ask. She wanted to chase after Shannon and stop her from leaving. *And then what?* She would take Shannon down with her if she stayed. She couldn't be so selfish, not again. She'd ruined Kelly's life, and there was no way she was ruining Shannon's too.

It was the right thing to do, even if it felt like the worst mistake she'd ever made.

CHAPTER ELEVEN

Bethany glanced across at her friend. Shannon looked deceptively happy. Her face was turned up towards the sun, and she smiled gently. Bethany knew she had lost weight. A lot of weight. There were shadows beneath her eyes now, and she rarely smiled anymore.

Things had been pretty hectic when she'd flown back from the UK. She was followed everywhere she went and ended up staying indoors for almost a month.

Bethany was worried about her best friend. Shannon stayed in bed, barely ate, and didn't return anybody's calls. She'd told Bethany it was because she wanted to lay low until the shit storm blew over. Bethany knew better. Jay had broken her best friend's heart.

"You feel like some lunch?" Bethany called over to the opposite lounger.

"No, I think I might go for a swim. It's hot."

"You need to eat, Shannon."

"Really? I think you're doing enough for both of us."

"Hey! I'm pregnant. I'm allowed to eat. Besides, Mark says he wants me big and fat because I look way too hot pregnant. He's worried other men will try and steal me away."

"He said that?" Shannon sat up quickly, frowning.

"No, I'm kidding. It's true he can't get enough of me right now."

"Gross, I don't want to hear about your sex life."

"Heterophobe."

"No, I'm not. Look, I don't have a problem with straight people as long as they keep it behind closed doors," Shannon joked. A rare thing, these days.

* * *

She'd officially come out a few weeks ago. It felt good to stand in front of people and say it, finally. It was strange, but she felt as though a huge weight had been lifted off her shoulders. It was a weight she had barely noticed because she'd become so used to it. Now it was gone, she finally realised just how heavy it really was.

She was lighter and freer—as long as she didn't think about Jay. She knew Bethany was worried about her, and she wanted to talk about what happened. That first month, Shannon couldn't bring herself to. She felt as though her world was sinking, dragging her into this huge pit of despair that she couldn't escape from.

"Am I allowed to talk about Jay yet?"

Just the mention of her name brought a fresh and exquisite stab of pain. Shannon sighed. "There really isn't a lot to talk about."

"No? You were going to come out publicly for her."

"Bullshit. Anyway, I was already outed."

"You know what I mean. Shannon, what happened?"

Maybe it was the look of kind concern on Bethy's face, or maybe it was just thinking about Jay again. Whatever the reason, Shannon felt fresh tears begin to fall as a terrible ache thudded in her heart.

"Shannon. I'm sorry." Bethy went to her and pulled her into a hug. "She really fucked you up?"

Shannon could only nod, her face pressed into Bethany. "Shannon, you know, she isn't worth it. If the whole paparazzi circus sent her running for the hills, then she isn't for you."

"That's not what it was," Shannon managed to mumble against Bethany.

"What do you mean?" Bethany held her back gently, by the shoulders. "I thought the paps scared her off."

"No. She...you know she killed her stepfather, right?"

"Sure, he raped her little sister. Fucker deserved it."

"She was worried about me—about my career if I was *associated* with her."

"So she let you go?"

"She thought she was saving me." Shannon laughed, bitterly.

"Wow. The two of you are really fucked up, aren't you?"

Shannon laughed then, a proper, full laugh. "We are. And that's why this is probably for the best."

"Oh, bullshit. Shannon, you've loved this woman for over ten years—"

"I barely even know her." Shannon stood, and walked to the edge of the pool.

"Shannon, that's not true. Something inside you recognised something in her, and knew you'd come home."

"It's too late, Bethy. She doesn't want me." Shannon could see all the way to the bottom of the pool. The water made lazy ripples, and she saw her face distorted in its reflection.

"If she feels the same as you—and I think she does, she'll never stop wanting you, Shannon."

* * *

At first, Jay was terrified of going into the village. When she finally worked up the courage, she braced herself for the sidelong glances and waited for people to cross the road to avoid her. None of those things happened. Everyone was exactly the same. The only difference—as far as she could tell—was she now had a freezer full of pies.

They'd come by slowly at first, and then, it felt like they were queuing up outside to give them to her.

Jay nearly cried with relief and gratitude at their kindness. Mrs Mackay was the one who finally did it. She'd popped by with another pie, and Jay burst into tears. She'd been so mortified and tried to turn away, but Mrs Mackay set the pie down and pulled her into a tight embrace.

Jay couldn't remember the last time that she let someone hold her while she'd cried, and here she was, doing it twice in as many months. She'd never really been one for tears in the first place. A small, cold part of herself always whispered only cowards cried. Well, she was a coward, wasn't she? That's what Shannon called her and how could she argue?

Jay sent her away and told her she didn't want to be with her. She'd let Shannon believe it was because of the fame thing—it was easier that way.

Jay couldn't count the number of times she'd almost called Shannon. She'd even dialled her number only to hang up before the call connected. She told herself it was better this way because they'd never have worked. *You've turned denial into an art form.*

Jay hadn't been able to watch Shannon's coming-out speech, but everyone in the village was talking about it. Jay pretended to be busy with the farm, busy with Alfie, busy with anything if it meant she didn't have to talk about Shannon, hear about Shannon, or see Shannon.

Behind her, she heard gravel crunching underfoot. She stood up from where she had been crouching to clean the Jeep's wheels—she washed her own car now, anything to keep busy, to keep moving.

"Hello, dear. Sorry to disturb you."

"No problem, Mrs Mackay. I was just about to go and put the kettle on."

"Oh, I can't stay, dear. I just came by with some news."

Jay studied her. She had a shiny glint in her eye which could only mean she'd unearthed a particularly good piece of gossip.

"Please say it isn't about me this time." Jay could hear the sulk in her own voice.

Mrs Mackay laughed. "I'm afraid so, though I think it'll be something you want to hear."

"I'm not convinced."

"Shush. I have to be at church in twenty minutes, so just listen. Your lady friend is coming to London."

"My lady friend?" Jay didn't understand.

"Shannon. Shannon's coming to the UK."

Jay felt something drop in her stomach. *Oh no, not again.* "How do you know this?" She tried to keep her voice calm.

"Never you mind how I know. She's coming on Thursday to London, and that's all that matters. I'll babysit."

"Mrs Mackay—"

"Now, you bloody well listen, and you listen good."

Jay was started by the tone in Mrs Mackay's voice. She clamped her mouth shut.

"Everybody knows the two of you are in love—except you, it seems. You were a bloody fool to send her away. You have a chance to get her back, so you'd better take it."

"What if she doesn't want me?"

"At least you'll know you tried, won't you? Honestly, Jay, I see you up at this farm day after day, moping around—"

"I'm not—"

"Moping around, thinking nobody knows how you feel about that girl. Well, we all think you were an idiot to send her away—"

"We all, who?"

"*Everyone.*" Mrs Mackay rolled her eyes. Unexpectedly she punched Jay on the arm.

"Stop being a fool and get her back."

Mrs Mackay turned without another word and walked away, leaving Jay staring after her, open-mouthed.

Jay went down to the summer house, unsure if she would find Henry at home. As she got closer, she saw him in his familiar position out front, reading.

Since Kelly went to rehab and after Shannon left, Jay made a habit of coming here to sit beside him. Often, they wouldn't speak. Jay found comfort just being in his calm, gentle presence. This time, she needed his advice, but she didn't know how to ask—didn't know how to begin.

As if reading her thoughts, Henry turned, his kind eyes upon her. "I wondered how long it would take you."

"What do you mean?"

"To come to your senses." Henry looked away again, across the fields. "I told you about my wife."

"Yes. It destroyed you."

He nodded, still looking away, perhaps seeing something other than the green and gold fields that stretched out for miles around. "But did I tell you I'd do it all again?"

"Even knowing how it turned out?" Jay asked quietly.

"Yes, even knowing how it turned out. How could I not? How could I turn my back on a love like that?"

Jay didn't notice the tears on her cheeks until she wiped at them.

"I'm scared it'll hurt," she whispered.

Henry smiled gently and took her hand. "You must be brave. Love is terrifying, and it always hurts. Even when it's good, it hurts. The trick is to make sure you find someone worth hurting for."

Jay said nothing as Henry squeezed her hand and held it between his on his lap. He had big hands. They both looked back across the fields.

* * *

Shannon leaned her head back and closed her eyes. All she could see was Jay's face, so she opened them again.

Carla handed her the note a week ago during a meeting to discuss her upcoming trip to the UK. She frowned as she passed it to Shannon, and when she read it, Shannon was surprised she gave it to her at all. Carla advised her not to come out, to deny the rumours completely. Shannon couldn't do it. She didn't want to hide anymore, so she refused.

Carla begged and pleaded, but Shannon held firm. When she handed her an envelope with a British postmark on it, Shannon was surprised—after her stomach stopped turning somersaults.

The note inside was brief and to the point, just like Jay herself. It simply read, *'I'm sorry, I was wrong. Please forgive me.'* There was a date and time and a place. Shannon didn't know what to do. She still hurt from Jay's rejection, and she wasn't sure if she could go through it all again.

And, she admitted to herself, she was angry. She'd bared her soul and taken a chance, and Jay had turned her away. Part of her wanted to punish her, wanted to show her how it felt to be rejected. *She already knows how it feels. She's had it her whole life.*

Shannon turned her face to the window and watched the world rush by. She still didn't know what to do.

* * *

She wasn't sure why she was here. *What if she doesn't come? Why would she?* Jay turned to study the pretty young things around her, with their shiny teeth and expensive-looking drinks.

She felt out of place and awkward as she rolled the bottle of beer between her hands and picked at the label. She'd been here so many times in the ten years since she first met Shannon. She'd sat in this very spot, waiting, hoping, for Shannon to come back and make the world right again. She hadn't come before, so why would she now? Especially after the way Jay had hurt her?

Jay turned back to the bar, took a long pull of her beer, and stared at her reflection in the polished wood.

"Can I buy you a drink?" A voice from behind, throaty and sweet and very, very sexy.

Jay sighed. "No, thanks, I'm waiting for someone."

"Really? What makes you think she'll show?"

"I don't know that she will," Jay admitted, "or that she'll even be interested in what I have to say."

"What is it that you're going to tell her?" the voice asked gently.

"That I was wrong. That I love her. That I'm sorry. I was coward. I wish I could take it all back."

"You hurt her." It wasn't a question.

Jay nodded and chanced a quick sideways glance at her companion. "I did. And I would do anything to take it back."

The woman on the other stool remained silent for so long Jay wondered if she had left. She couldn't bring herself to look up and check.

"Can I...can I buy you a drink?"

"Honey, my drink costs eighty pounds a glass," the woman said, and Jay closed her eyes with relief and smiled.

"You can buy your own drink then." Her voice sounded scratchy to her own ears.

Shannon laughed beside her. She reached out and gripped Jay's shoulder. She turned Jay to face her. "What's going on, Jay? Why did you ask me here?"

Jay met Shannon's eyes. "I made a mistake. I thought I was protecting you by sending you away. I was wrong."

"I can take care of myself."

"I know." Jay grinned. "I watched you on that talk show telling everyone you were gay. It took a lot of guts." Jay sipped from her bottle of beer and laughed when Shannon took it off her and drank.

"I'm glad I did it. I'm just sorry you got dragged into the whole mess."

Jay shrugged. "I shouldn't have sent you away."

"You keep saying that. What does it mean though, Jay? I thought we were in love. I thought you wanted to make it work. Then you told me to go. I didn't hear from you for weeks, and then I get your cryptic note."

Jay sighed. She wanted Shannon back, and she was worried she was making a mess of the whole thing. "I don't know what to say except that I'm sorry. I was a coward. I love you, Shannon. I want you back. Please give me another chance."

Shannon was silent, and Jay braced herself for rejection. Shannon took another sip of the beer she'd commandeered.

"What about the next time something tough comes up? I'm in the public eye, Jay. There'll be more reporters, more stories, more intrusion into your carefully constructed life. How do I know you won't push me away again?"

Jay was waiting for this. "I love you."

"Is it enough?"

Jay didn't know the answer to that. She didn't know if she could live her life in the spotlight like Shannon and lose all her privacy. She was willing to give it a shot though. "I waited over ten years for you to come back to me, Shannon. I can't promise it'll be easy living this public life with you. Or that I won't get freaked out from time to time. I want to try though."

Shannon smiled, and the sadness that had surrounded Jay since she'd left began to lift. "What the hell," Shannon said. "Let's do it."

Jay jumped up from her stool and pulled Shannon into a hug. "Thank you."

"I do have one condition though, Jay. It's non-negotiable."

Jay stepped back and released Shannon. She was prepared to do whatever it took. "Okay." She nodded.

"You need to watch at least one of my movies. It's hurting my ego that you haven't seen any of them."

Jay laughed. "I'll even buy a TV to watch them on."

"Attagirl."

Jay slipped her arms around Shannon's waist and pulled her in. She kissed her gently on the lips and breathed in the scent of her. Finally, after all these years, she felt like she had all her broken pieces back together again. She was happy.

EPILOGUE

July 2017

Shannon smiled as Alfie chased Joe across the lawn. In the lounger next to her, Kelly laughed. "He loves that dog."

"I think the feeling is mutual," Shannon replied.

Kelly was doing much better. She'd put on weight and seemed less fragile every day. She was still prickly, but the anger was gone, and Shannon was growing to like her.

After finishing rehab, Kelly moved in with Jay. It made sense because Jay was still officially Alfie's guardian, and it allowed her to be close to him while at the same time being free from responsibility so she could get her life back on track. Shannon had been there when the social worker had given them the good news about Alfie being able to stay with Jay—she had to jump through a lot of hoops because of her record, but she didn't seem to mind a single one.

Kelly was back at school, studying to be a social worker. She joked about how strange it would be to sit on the other side of the fence for a change. Shannon could tell it meant a lot to her and her battered confidence.

Shannon waved as Jay walked over, balancing a baby on her hip. She looked up and squinted into the sun. "Where did you find her?"

Jay sat on the end of the lounger and passed the baby to Shannon. "Bethany asked me to take her because it was difficult trying to look through your wardrobe and hold Ellie at the same time."

"What?" Shannon cried.

Jay and Kelly burst into laughter.

"She'd better not be."

Shannon handed Ellie back to Jay and hurried inside before Bethy made off with her summer wardrobe.

Shannon had flown Bethany and Mark over for their anniversary which happily coincided with Alfie's birthday. They spoke every day on the phone, but it wasn't the same as having them here.

Shannon was due to start shooting her come-back movie—as it was being billed—in a few months, and this would be the last opportunity for her to spend time with the people she loved for a while.

Upstairs in the bedroom, she spotted Bethy pulling on one of her awards gowns. She didn't even have the grace to look contrite at being caught.

"Jay ratted me out," she said instead.

"Of course she did. She knows to stay on my good side."

"I'll bet."

Bethy unzipped the dress and sat down on the bed. "Sorry I started without you."

"It's fine. See anything you want to keep—I mean borrow?"

Bethany punched her playfully on the arm. "Not yet, but the day is young. I wanted to talk to you anyway."

Shannon looked at Bethy's serious face and rolled her eyes. "What now?"

"You start shooting your new movie soon. How are you feeling?"

"Fine."

"Fine? You aren't worried about the possibility of seeing Corin?"

Shannon waved her hand dismissively. "Last I heard, she was in Argentina. Naked and afraid."

Bethy laughed.

"Okay, maybe I'm a little nervous. It's been a long time. Plus, since I'm off the radar, me and Jay get to live a normal life."

"Are you worried she'll freak again?"

Shannon shook her head. A lot had changed this last year, including Jay. "No, she's solid. It's me. I'm not sure if I want to make movies anymore. I'll be away for months."

"Jay will visit though, right?"

"When she can. If she can get a visa with her criminal record."

"Well, see how it goes. You don't have to decide anything right now."

"I know. Jay has fallen in love with Ellie, by the way."

Bethy looked smug. "Of course she did. My baby is seriously cute."

Shannon laughed. "She certainly is."

"Oh, I get it."

"What?" Shannon frowned.

"You're broody."

"No, I'm not."

"Yes, you are."

"Maybe a little," Shannon admitted.

"Right. A little. Is Jay broody too?"

"Definitely."

"So shoot the movie, then come back and one of you can get yourselves knocked up."

Shannon laughed. Trust Bethany to make it sound so simple.

"You waited ten years to get with Jay. If you leave it another ten years before you have a baby...well." Bethy scrunched her face and nodded at Shannon's crotch.

Shannon burst into laughter and hugged her friend.

About the Author

Eden lives in London with her partner and their small, earless rescue cat. She runs her own business, and when she's not working or writing, can usually be found rowing up and down the Thames.

Twitter: http://www.twitter.com/EdenDarry

Other books by this author

Strangers

Bitten

NineStar Press, LLC

www.ninestarpress.com

www.ingramcontent.com/pod-product-compliance
Lightning Source LLC
Chambersburg PA
CBHW020334260626
47156CB00004B/1524